The
WOMAN
As GOOD as
the MAN

MEN WHO WROTE ABOUT WOMEN

Marilyn Williamson and James Turner, Series Editors

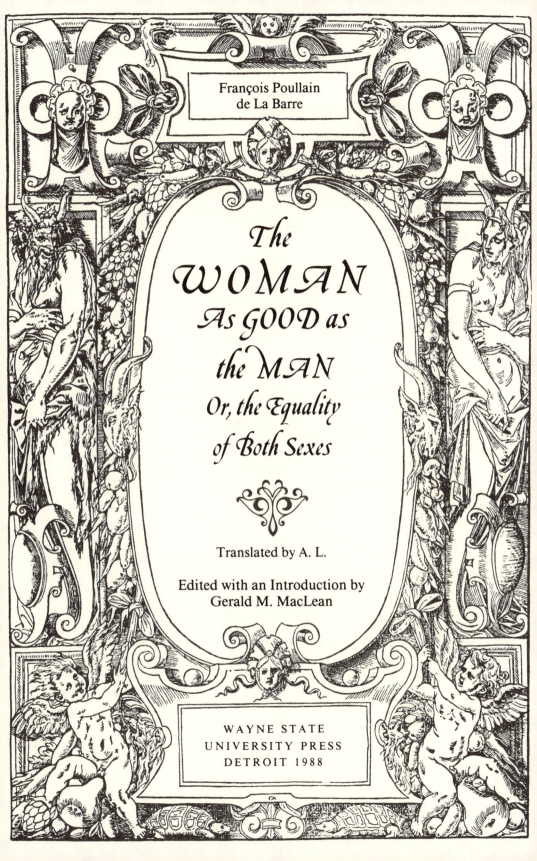

François Poullain
de La Barre

The WOMAN As GOOD as the MAN

Or, the Equality of Both Sexes

Translated by A. L.

Edited with an Introduction by
Gerald M. MacLean

WAYNE STATE
UNIVERSITY PRESS
DETROIT 1988

The Woman As Good as the Man was first published as *De l'egalité des deux sexes* in Paris in 1673. The text of this edition is based on the English translation by A. L. published in 1677 by Nathaniel Brooks.

Copyright © 1988 by Wayne State University Press, Detroit, Michigan 48202. All rights are reserved.
No part of this book may be reproduced without formal permission.

92 91 90 89 88   5 4 3 2 1

Library of Congress Cataloging-in-Publication Data

Poulain de La Barre, François, 1647–1723.
    [De l'égalité des deux sexes. English]
    The woman as good as the man, or, The equality of both sexes / François Poullain de La Barre ; translated by A.L. ; edited with introduction by Gerald M. MacLean.
        p. cm. — (Men who wrote about women)
    Based on the English translation of: De l'égalité des deux sexes. 1673.
    Includes index.
    ISBN 0–8143–1953–X (alk. paper). ISBN 0–8143–1954–8 (pbk. : alk. paper)
    1. Women—Early works to 1800. 2. Feminism—Early works to 1800. 3. Women's rights—Early works to 1800. I. MacLean, Gerald M., 1952–   . II. Title. III. Title: Woman as good as the man. IV. Title: Equality of both sexes. V. Series.
HQ1201.P6413 1988
305.4′2—dc19   88–10808
                                                                  CIP

For Donna Landry

Contents

Editorial Preface

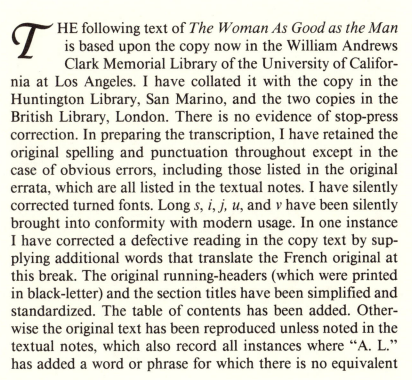

*T*HE following text of *The Woman As Good as the Man* is based upon the copy now in the William Andrews Clark Memorial Library of the University of California at Los Angeles. I have collated it with the copy in the Huntington Library, San Marino, and the two copies in the British Library, London. There is no evidence of stop-press correction. In preparing the transcription, I have retained the original spelling and punctuation throughout except in the case of obvious errors, including those listed in the original errata, which are all listed in the textual notes. I have silently corrected turned fonts. Long *s, i, j, u,* and *v* have been silently brought into conformity with modern usage. In one instance I have corrected a defective reading in the copy text by supplying additional words that translate the French original at this break. The original running-headers (which were printed in black-letter) and the section titles have been simplified and standardized. The table of contents has been added. Otherwise the original text has been reproduced unless noted in the textual notes, which also record all instances where "A. L." has added a word or phrase for which there is no equivalent in the original. A further selection of phrases from the second (1676) Paris edition of *De l'egalité* (upon which "A. L.'s" translation is demonstrably based) are also included to illustrate instances where the English deviates from, or expressively renders, the original. Other examples are discussed in the introduction.

I would like to thank John Bidwell at the Clark Library for first drawing my attention to the English translation of Poullain de La Barre, and Marilyn Williamson, who encouraged the project from its inception. At various stages in the preparation of the introduction, Marie-Florine Bruneau, Moira Ferguson, Catherine Gallagher, Elaine Hobby, Catherine Lafarge, Donna Landry, Martha Malamud, Felicity Nussbaum, Gayatri Spivak, and Rachel Weil have helped me track references and avoid many obvious errors. Those remaining are, of course, due to my own obstinacy.

Introduction

*T*HIS edition of François Poullain de La Barre's *De l'égalité des deux sexes* is based upon *The Woman As Good as the Man,* which was published by Nathaniel Brooks in 1677, "translated into *English* by A. L." Of Poullain de La Barre, whom Simone de Beauvoir considered "the leading feminist of the age,"[1] the archival record has been well served with recent studies by Marie-Louise Stock, Bernard Magné, Madeleine Alcover, and the *Corpus* 1 group of essays that appeared in conjunction with the recent reprint of *De l'égalité* in the series Corpus des oeuvres de philosophie en langue française (Paris: Fayard, 1984).[2] So of his life and works we need recall only the broadest of outlines here.

Poullain de La Barre (1647–1723)

Born of well-to-do parents in Paris in July 1647, Poullain was an able scholar, who attended the Sorbonne, took clerical orders, and might have expected to rise to high clerical office. But in or around 1667, he came under the influence of the philosophy of Descartes, which was gaining ground at the time among intellectual groups in Paris. Cartesian rationalism so appealed to him that he abandoned the scholastic theology still dominating the official discourse of church and university and left Paris in order to teach ordinary people the truth that, he now felt certain, was to be found by direct study of the New Testament. Nothing is known, precisely, of his whereabouts until 1679 when, it appears, he was living at the Collège de Fortet on a lifetime annuity. At the end of the next year, he was appointed to the curacy of La Flamengrie in Picardy.

It was during these years of obscurity that his three most important works were written and published in quick succession. *De l'égalité des deux sexes, Discours physique et moral, où l'on voit l'importance de se défaire des Préjugez* was published by Jean DuPuis in Paris sometime after July of 1673. *De l'education des Dames pour la conduite de l'esprit dans les sciences et dans les moeurs* appeared from the same publisher a year later. In the next year DuPuis also published Poullain's *De l'excellence des Hommes, Contre l'égalité des sexes.* This title, however, may prove misleading since the work is highly rhetorical in design, offering counterarguments to *De l'égalité* in order to demonstrate their untenability. Of Poullain's commitment to a rationalistic critique of social formations, particularly with regard to the equality of men and women, there can be little doubt.[3]

But such ideas were radical and socially subversive. Although Poullain's works were published anonymously, his views on scriptural authority, on liberty of conscience, on religious images, and on the eucharist made him suspect among local church authorities. In 1685 he left La Flamengrie for the much smaller curacy of Saint-Jean Baptiste de Versigny but not before obtaining a certificate from his bishop attesting to the orthodoxy of his views. Nevertheless, he stayed on in this appointment only until 1682 when, threatened by the local church with a warrant of imprisonment, he resigned his ministry and returned to Paris. At the end of the same year, feeling no longer secure either in conscience or in body, he left Catholic France for Protestant Geneva where he was well received, partly on account of the bishop's certificate. A little over a year later, on 5 January 1690, he married Marie Ravier, daughter of a member of the Council of State, with whom he had two children. But despite the respectability and importance of his new family connections, Poullain again found himself under the suspicions of local ecclesiastical authorities. In January 1696 he was accused of Socinianism—the view that Christ was human and not divine—but was able to satisfy a panel of theology professors that his faith was beyond reproach.

During these early years in Geneva, Poullain may have supported himself and his family by teaching the French language. His *Essai des remarques particulières sur la langue françoise pour la ville de Genève* was published there in 1691. In any case, the scandals regarding his possible heterodoxy died down sufficiently by 1708 for him to be appointed master at the Collège de Gèneve, where he taught history, rhetoric, and New Testament Greek. Apart from a reprimand for not keeping strict enough discipline in the classroom, Poullain seems to have kept out of trouble from then on. In 1720 he published his final work, *La Doctrine des protestants sur la liberté de lire l'Écriture Sainte,* in the city that, four years earlier, had granted him citizenship. He died on 4 May 1723, at age 76.

In his book on women's education, Poullain writes that his commitment to women's equality originated in his engagement with Cartesian method (see Alcover, *Poullain de La Barre,* p. 16). This seems no reason to view what in Poullain's major works reads like a personal commitment to exposing the prejudices embedded in traditional notions about women as being any the less genuine. But whatever the biographical truth may be, his theoretical investigation in *De l'égalité* of the extent to which our notion of *woman* is a social construct based upon vulgar prejudice rather than historical fact constitutes one of the most important contributions to feminist thinking in the era before Mary Wollstonecraft.

"A. L." and Archibald Lovell

Accordingly, we might have wished that the English version of *De l'égalité* had been undertaken by a woman. Unfortunately a satisfactory case cannot be made for either of the two obvious women candidates who were writers of the period with appropriate initials.[4] "Mrs." Anne Levingston appears as the author of two very rare and brief tracts published in 1654 and 1655 in which she defends herself from accusations of fraud.[5] Since these are the only occasions on which she appears as a writer, there would seem to be no reason to link her with the "A. L." who made an English translation of Poullain's *De l'égalité*. Anne de La Roche-Guilhem, however, is a more promising possibility, since her name has been associated with several books, in both French and English, that appeared around the same time as *The Woman*. Her *Rare en Tout: Comedie* and her *Asteria and Tamberlain* —"rendred into English by E. C., Esq."—were both published in London in 1677.[6] But all of the works by, or attributed to, La Roche-Guilhem—including her *Histoire des Favorites* (1697),[7] a collection of stories about exceptional women—are of a distinctly romantic, rather than philosophical, nature. And since she is not accredited with having translated any of her own works, there is, presumably, no reason to imagine she would have translated the work of someone else for a publisher with whom she was at no time associated.

In all likelihood, the "A. L." who translated Poullain's *De l'égalité* was Archibald Lovell, a rather shadowy figure responsible for a number of translations, mostly from French writers, between 1677 and 1687. In his *Athenae Oxonienses,* Anthony à Wood informs us that the 1685 translation of George Bate's *Elenchus Motuum Nuperorum in Anglia: Or, A short Historical Account of the Rise and Progress of the Late Troubles in England,* published by Abel Swalle, was by "one *A. Lovel* M. A. of *Cambridge . . .* but not well done.[8] À Wood evidently knew more about Lovell than he was willing to tell us since he adds, "in which year [1685] he had two translations of other mens works extant, the mentioning of which, as being not pertinent, is now to be omitted."[9] But Archibald is not among the Lovells who appear in the *Alumni Cantabrigienses.*[10] The biographical record concerning Archibald Lovell's institutional affiliations is marked with further confusion. In his one originally composed work, *A Summary of Material Heads Which may be Enlarged and Improved into a Compleat Answer To Dr. Burnet's Theory of the Earth* (1696), Lovell identifies himself as *"Brother* and *Pensioner* of the *Charter-House"* (Sig. A2ᵛ). But, although he must have been an old man to have warranted a pensioner's place at this hospital, he does not seem to have died there.[11]

To *A Summary* we are indebted for two other vague biographical details. At some time in his life he went to sea, sailing as far into the tropics as the fifteenth and sixteenth parallels north, and in his later years he was blind (pp. 10, 25–26). But more significantly, we can also infer that Lovell was a man, like Poullain, of considerable personal courage and intellectual integrity who was committed to the rationalist method associated with the "new" science of empirical analysis. For *A Summary* is nothing less than an attack on a celebrated work by the man who was in command of the very institution to which Lovell, at the time he published this work, owed his livelihood.

When Thomas Burnet's *The Theory of the Earth: Containing an Account of the Original of the Earth. And of all the General Changes Which it hath already undergone, Or is to undergo Till the Consummation of Things* (1684) had first appeared in a Latin version in 1681, it attracted the admiration of Charles II.[12] In 1685, the year the king died, Burnet was appointed to the mastership of the Charterhouse, a former Carthusian monastery that, since the dissolution, had served as both a hospital for *"Fourscore ancient Men,* who have been formerly in the Wars, and been serviceable to their King and Country: or else decay'd Merchants, whose Estates have been swallowed up in the Deep, or aged and poor Householders, who have formerly lived in a fair esteem with the World"[13] and as a school for forty boys. With the Glorious Revolution of 1688, Burnet was appointed chaplain in ordinary to the new king, William of Orange, and was expected to be appointed archbishop. But the growing controversy over the orthodoxy of the final version of his *Theory,* which appeared in 1689, cost him his bishopric, despite the dedication to Queen Mary. This is the man whom Lovell, though certainly "ancient," presumably destitute, and by his own account blind, bravely set out to contradict in his *Summary.* It is hardly surprising that in the dedication to "The Governours of the Charter-House," Lovell should have craved *"Your Lordships* favourable Protection, in a little Ramble that I have made to the Press" (Sig. A2).

Lovell's critique begins with Burnet's argument that the account of the flood in the Bible cannot be true since there is insufficient water in the universe to drown the Earth. In reply, Lovell sets out "to shew, how without a Miracle, Water enough may be had in the World, to bring a Flood upon the Earth, and drown it in the manner *Moses* has related it" (p. 2). Burnet's theologicomoralistic solution to this problem—that divine retribution included destroying the formerly smooth sphere of the earth, causing the surface to collapse inwards and so be flooded by the water that was originally contained inside—is rejected by Lovell in favor of an account that reconciles known physical laws with the biblical account. Demonstrating familiarity with the law of gravity, Lovell's argument bears the stamp of modern rationalism throughout. If, according to the Mosaic account, "the World was overwhelmed by a Flood, and the Waters mounted Fifteen Cubits high, over the tops of the highest Mountains," Lovell sets out to show "how it may be done by Natural Causes, without any Miracle" (p. 7). Arguing by analogy between the earth and the human body that water circulates through the land as blood does through the flesh, he offers as empirical evidence his own observations that water in waterspouts can be raised higher than land by natural means (pp. 7–10). When he turns to Burnet directly, it is by way of repeating one of the crucial arguments of the age. "Instead of proving his Doctrine of an Egg-World by Natural Reason, which indeed he could not do, He endeavours to Establish it, by the Authority of the Ancients who have compar'd the World to an Egg" (p. 23).

On the superior claims to truth of natural reason over the authority of the ancients, Poullain would have been in total agreement. This is, after all, the very strategy upon which his critique of received notions of women in *De l'egalité* is based. But the commitment to a similar intellectual position hardly goes very far by way of proving that Lovell was the "A. L." responsible for *The Woman*. It only indicates that he would have been in sympathy with Poullain's enterprise. For evidence that Lovell was the "A. L." in question, we must turn to the other works that bear his name or have been attributed to him.

In addition to *A Summary,* there are eight other works that carry the name "A. Lovell" or "A. Lovel." All of them are translations from contemporary French writers, and many of them display a significant engagement with the rationalist method associated with the new science in general and with Cartesianism in particular. One of these, François Antoine Pomey's *Indiculus Universalis; Or, The universe in Epitome, wherein the Names of almost all the Works of Nature, of all Arts and Sciences, with their most necessary Terms, are in English, Latine & French, Methodically and distinctly digested,* was evidently intended to serve a pedagogical purpose. It is dedicated to "the Right-Honorable CHARLES Lord Beauclair, Baron of Hedington, Earl of Durford, and Master of the Hawks to His Majesty," who was, presumably, young at the time despite his titles since Lovell writes "I am confident you will, to your satisfaction, find . . . a concomittant help that will, *aequis passibus,* wait on you until Your *Lordship* be grown up to such maturity of Knowledge and Merit. . . ." (Sig. A2ᵛ).

Other translations by Lovell show a similar interest in the new learning. They include an ethnographic work— Richard Simons's *The Critical History of the Religions and Customs of the Eastern Nations* (London: Henry Faithorne & John Kersey, 1685); a scientific work—Isaac Vossius's *A Treatise Concerning the Motion of the Seas and Winds* (London: Henry Brome, 1676); a translation of a rather unnervingly graphic guide to surgeons—François Tolet's *A Treatise of Lithotomy: Or, of the Extraction of the Stone out of the Bladder,* which William Cademan published in 1683; an early example of what we would call *literary theory*—Renée Rapin's *Reflections Upon Ancient and Modern History* (1678) also published by Cademan;[14] and *The Travels of Monsieur de Thevenot Into the Levant,* a large folio published by Henry Faithorne, J. Adamson, C. Skegnes, and T. Newborough in 1687. Books such as these were very much the product of the new scientific method that favored quantitative analysis based upon empirical observation over the old scholastic emphases upon the received wisdom of the ancient philosophers and biblical commentators.[15]

Pomey's *Indiculus* appeared two years after *The Woman* and was published by Robert Harford "at the Angel in Cornhill near the Royal Exchange." This advertisement provides the crucial link between Lovell and the "A. L." who translated Poullain, since it refers to the same shop from which Nathaniel Brooks sold *The Woman* (see title page). From the same address, Harford published two other French works translated by "A. L." who, there is reason to think, was also Lovell, suggesting that he had something of a steady, though by no means regular, professional connection with this publisher. *The Military Duties of the Officers of Cavalry, Containing the way of exercising the Horse, According to the practise of this present time* (1678), "Written Originally in French, by the Sieur De la Fontaine," has been ascribed to Lovell in the *The British Library General Catalogue*.[16] The same source also names Lovell as the "A. L." who translated Harford's publication of the Abbé de Montfaucon de Villars's *The Count de Gabalis,* the Rosicrucian romance immortalized for English readers in Pope's revisions to *The Rape of the Lock.* In editing Pope's poem for the "Twickenham" edition, Geoffrey Tillotson accepts that Lovell was the "A. L." in question here.[17] And certainly the translator's sceptical disavowal of belief in the system being put forth is in keeping with what we know of Lovell's personal opinions.[18]

Since none of the other works published during the second half of the seventeenth century listed in the *Catalogue* of

the British Library or in Wing's *Short-Title Catalogue* as by
or translated by "A. L." provide either a candidate more
likely than Lovell to have translated Poullain or any evidence
to the contrary,[19] the connection between Lovell and the publishing house of Harford and Brooks would seem to be about
as conclusive a piece of evidence as we are likely to find.
Moreover, the little we know about Lovell goes a long way to
confirming the attribution. Like Poullain he was personally
committed to advancing the cause of modern thought. Lovell
constantly, regularly emphasizes in the prefaces to the works
he translated, the love of learning and the desire to promote
what the French had to say. The Preface to Thévenot's *Travels* offers a typical formulation when Lovell praises "the worthy Traveller who ended his Days in endeavouring to promote Knowledge and improve Learning" (Sig. a^v). And later
he commends Thévenot's learning in no uncertain terms that
surely tell us something of his own interests and aspirations.
"He attain'd," Lovell writes, "to great knowledge in Natural
Philosophy, Geometry, Astronomy, and all the Mathematicks; and had especially studied the Philosophy of *Descartes,*
rather that he might examine Natural Effects in their Principles, than Magisterially dictate and decide, as those who now
a days make a shew of that Philosophy commonly do" (Sig.
b2^v). As a professional translator, he seems to have been
mostly engaged in making works of a rationalistic and scientific bias available to English readers. And, like Poullain, he
was prepared to risk his personal well-being in the cause of
intellectual enlightenment.

Finally, the case for Lovell as Poullain's translator is
buttressed by the style of *The Woman* which, both as an example of English prose and as a translation, conforms with
Lovell's stated opinions and practice elsewhere. "A genuine
and simple style, such as can raise a distinct Idea in the mind
of the Reader, is the proper style for particular and exact Relations of things." This formula, again from Lovell's preface
to Thévenot (Sig. b), conforms with the principles set out for
English prose of the new age by Thomas Sprat in his *History
of the Royal Society* (1667).[20] It also goes a long way towards

describing Lovell's style and practice as a translator. Indeed, Lovell typically follows this stylistic principle so closely that he earned, as we have seen, a rebuke from Anthony à Wood, who was himself more prone to the old-fashioned florid style of the earlier part of the century. As a translator, Lovell's habitual adherence to the text before him also drew the censure of no less a figure than Samuel Taylor Coleridge who, in his marginalia to Lovell's translation of Thévenot, frequently complains that Lovell has stuck too closely to the French. Where Lovell has given us, concerning Turkish women, "Their Habit is fit to make them seem proper," Coleridge has glossed "A French Idiom *worded* instead of *translated.* We should say, 'There [*sic*] Dress is becoming, & covers defects &c.'"[21]

The Woman and De l'égalité

Leaving aside, now, the case for identifying Lovell as the "A. L." in question, we may nevertheless notice that the English version of Poullain's *De l'égalité* does, for the most part, constitute a *wording* or (in Dryden's term) a *metaphrase* —that species of translation that consists in "turning an author word by word, and line by line, from one language into another."[22] As a translation, *The Woman* exemplifies this process of metaphrase by following, with very few exceptions, the paragraphing and sentence structure of the original French. "A. L." almost certainly based the translation on the second DuPuis edition of 1676. Collation of the 1673 and 1676 DuPuis editions shows that the text of 1676 differs frequently in orthographic accidentals but very seldom in substantives. The opening sentence of the preface, however, reads "IL n'y a rien de plus délicat que de s'expliquer sur le sujet des Femmes" (Sig. ai), whereas the text of 1673 reads "IL n'y a rien de plus délicat de s'expliquer sur les Femmes" (Sig. aii). The opening of *The Woman* clearly follows the later version, so the following discussion is based upon comparison with the 1676 text.

Staying as close to this text as syntax and idiom would allow, "A. L." (or the publisher) omits only the marginal annotations that appear in both the 1673 and 1676 French versions. In the few instances where *The Woman* strays from this general rule, it is invariably to add weight or clarity to the original, or to avoid confusion because of sociocultural differences between France and England during the seventeenth century. "A. L." is not, for example, very keen on translating the French *état* into the English word *state*. The term is either avoided or expanded into a longer phrase that anglicizes, as it were, the notion of the state. The French "gouvernement des États" (p. 22) is given as "the Administration of Publick Government" (p. 70) while "L'ETABLISSEMENT des États ne se pût faire" (p. 23) becomes "States and Common-Wealths could not be established" (p. 71). In either case the translation avoids any inappropriate connotations lurking in the minds of English readers who, in 1677, would have been certain to remember the political turmoil which can result from disputes over such matters as that of the *state*. Where *état* is linked to women's power, however, "A. L." seems prepared to use *state* (e.g. pp. 72, 98, 112), though it also appears thus in relation to the authority of the prince (p. 95). When, however, the French invites us to think of civil war—"ce n'a esté que pour éviter de tomber en guerre civile" (p. 26)—"A. L." steers clear of the memory and offers the dismissively humorous "It was only that they might prevent the People from falling together by the Ears" (p. 72).

Not all deviations from the original are political in character. Some are cultural, such as the greater tendency of the French language to employ abstract terms and conceptions where seventeenth-century English preferred a more concrete idiom. "Les jeunes hommes au sortit de leurs études" (p. 38), for instance, becomes the more graphic "young men when they come new off of the press" (p. 76), "précisement" (p. 44) becomes "to a hair" (p. 78), "malgré nous" (p. 229) is similarly rendered with a body part as "in spight of our Teeth" (p. 145), and "n'en diroit mot" (p. 242) is given "he would not open his Mouth" (p. 149). The French "de réprendre" (p.

181), for which Cotgrave's *Dictionarie* (1611) gives "to resume, receive, take back . . . reprehend, blame, check, rebuke,"[23] becomes "to spill and shed" (p. 128), indicating "A. L."'s adherence to the general sense of the original. On occasion, this tendency to favor the concrete in the English leads "A. L." to employ personification not found in the original as when he gives us "Knowledge being but the hand-Maid to Vertue" (p. 85) where Poullain wrote "la science se doit uniquement rapporter à la vertue" (p. 63), or "It is Death that must discharge them" (p. 87) for "C'est pour le reste de leur vie" (p. 69). This tendency to favor concrete formulas or graphic figures of speech over abstractions adds further vigor to Poullain's ironic contempt for pagans by drawing out the original formula describing Egyptian priests—"s'amusoient ensemble à parler" (p. 27)—into a more colloquial phrase— "busied themselves in chatting together" (p. 72)—that postpones the effect by setting up a slide from *busied* to the trivializing *chatting*. The original relies entirely on the initial term *s'amusoient* to carry the effect. As a general rule, where "A. L." varies from the principle of metaphrase, it is to add idiomatic weight—via imagery or metaphor—to an abstract formulation in the original.

Sometimes the adherence to the original does lead to odd or awkward English, the sort of thing Coleridge would have deplored. *Contre-temps* (p. 225) is worded as *cross Times* (p. 143), and *goust* (p. 230), which Cotgrave gives as *taste,* appears as *Gusto* (p. 145). Only very occasionally does the English make little sense, as when "pour prendre des mesures avec elles" (p. 242) is literally given as "to consult about her Measures with them" (p. 149). But usually "A. L." avoids being too servile in sticking needlessly close to Poullain's original. He avoids, for example, the Frenchman's emphatic use of multiple negatives when this would lead to garbled English. "Les manieres qu'on trouva qui Seoient le mieux, ne furent point negligées: & ceux qui estoient sous le mesme Prince ne manquerent pas de se conformer à luy" (p. 29) becomes "The Fashions that were the most decent, were presently followed; and they that were under the same Prince, strove to conform themselves to his Mode" (p. 73).

Generally, "A. L."'s care to keep the sense clear and precise accounts for those instances where words or phrases are added that have no equivalent in the French. Unlike the examples just discussed, all of these are listed in the textual notes. But we may notice here that, without distorting the original or changing the sentence structure, these additional words or phrases usually add emphasis to a point (see examples listed at textual notes 30, 31, 46, 49, 52), or have the effect of enlivening a phrase, as when "des plus délicates parties du corps" (p. 150) is expanded to "the most ticklish and delicate Parts of the Body" (p. 117) or "luy mettre levent, la poussiere, le Soleil en face" (p. 170) is broken up and supplemented to give us "put the wind and dust in his teeth, and the Sun in his face" (p. 124).

But given the argument of the work at hand, perhaps the most important variations from the French involve the manner in which "A. L." has set about translating gender-specific phrases and pronouns. Sometimes the English usage contributes to the feminist argument by its greater precision or edge, as when "les gens" (p. 9) appears in English as "these Blades" (p. 66). At other times, however, "A. L." seems to have lapsed into using the generic male when translating "tout le monde" (p. 215) as "all men" (p. 140), or "le corps humain" (p. 57) as "the body of man" (p. 83).

Sometimes the greater specificity as to gender in the translation actually dulls what is more accurately grasped by the French—that the issue at hand is an ideological matter, something in which all are potentially complicit regardless of gender. For the central argument of Poullain's work involves demystification of traditional opinions regarding women. "Presque tout," he writes, "ce qu'il y a eu de gens qui on passé pour sçavans & qui ont parlé des femmes, n'ont rien dit à leur avantage" (pp. 12–13). "A. L."'s translation is more pithy and specific but loses the sense of scrutinizing a general cultural condition: "Most part of Men, who have passed for Learned, have not said anything to the advantage of Women" (p. 67). This difficulty, the loss of a general cultural critique, most commonly arises in relation to the nonspecific impersonal pronoun *on,* which "A. L." normally translates to mean *men,* though on one occasion he uses the available English form *one* (p. 77) and on another, where the sense obviously demands it, *Woman:* "On ne peut apprendre" (p. 149) becoming "A *Woman* cannot Learn" (p. 117).

For the most part, though, *The Woman* demonstrates the principles of metaphrase—close translation that follows the original word-for-word, sentence by sentence—combined with (as in the last example) the translator's close and detailed attention to meaning. The examples I have discussed here are, for the most part, exceptional instances that arise from sociocultural differences between France and England or from the virtual impossibility of translating French grammar and syntax into clear idiomatic English that remains faithful to the sense and structure of the original. Other instances are provided in the textual notes. *The Woman* may not be a hitherto undiscovered gem of seventeenth-century English prose style, but it renders Poullain's important argument concerning the concept and status of women forcefully and accurately in the "genuine and simple style, such as can raise a distinct Idea in the mind of the Reader." Let us turn, then, to that argument and the contexts in which it appeared and was received.

The Woman As Good as the Man: Some Contemporary English Contexts

In 1982, the late Joan Kelly warned of a dangerous tendency, especially in Anglo-American "monographic work," to imagine that feminist theory began only 150 years ago. The danger is in forgetting, as it were, the important prowoman debates generated from the pioneering work of Christine de Pisan in early fifteenth-century France, which continued, in both French and English, until the French Revolution.[24] This forgetting is a danger not only to feminist theorists and historians but to any scholar or reader interested in early modern literature and history since, as Kelly shows, these early "reactive" debates against misogyny in France played no small part in the growth of an international bourgeois ideology that proved capable of withstanding the ethical, intellectual, and political impact of postfeudal upheavals to emerge triumphant under capitalism within the formations of the liberal state apparatus. Forgetting the *querelle* has also encouraged a forgetting of the arguments it advanced concerning ideological entrapment and gender construction within a dominantly masculinist culture. These are arguments that remain relevant in our times.

The Woman pursues topics characteristic of the *querelle.* Women's inferiority to men is exposed as a social construct as, indeed, is the very concept of *woman.* The first part inveighs against vulgar opinions by showing how popular notions of women are socialized prejudice. The second part takes on poets, orators, historians, lawyers, and philosophers who have given intellectual weight to antiwoman prejudice by falsely assigning it to nature rather than culture. In the new manner of rationalist empiricism, *The Woman* argues that women are not only capable of better education and more responsible public employment than currently available to them but that they are eminently suited to these and other activities from which men have traditionally excluded them. Sex and gender are not, we learn, the same thing. Sexual distinctions are of concern to anatomists and artists but are void of ethical content. Indeed, what we unthinkingly accept to be differences of gender are seldom more than the signs of social and educational systems that have defined *masculine* and *feminine* for us. The self is largely a social construction in respect of "the Relation of Sex, Age, Fortune and Employment, wherein we are placed in Society" (p. 137). We are slowly coming to rediscover these arguments in our concerns over essentialism, subject formation and the broad social critique inherent in much structuralist and poststructuralist theory.[25]

For the modern reader, then, there are two likely directions leading to an interest in *The Woman:* an historical interest in the culture of early modern England, and a (no doubt) allied political interest in arguments concerning women's liberation. Since these lines of approach converge in this single text, we need not dwell on their differences here beyond recalling again that general inclination that Joan Kelly noticed to "think of feminism, and certainly of feminist theory, as taking rise in the nineteenth and twentieth centuries" (p. 4) and the more alarming apolitical tendency of traditional social historians to ignore the conditions of the subject in an "objective" pursuit of truth. If politicizing the personal has sometimes encouraged the reification of the self, individuated by reason of its self-division, its subjectivity formed out of alienation, then the tenacity of unreflexive empiricism—which happily affirms the "natural order" of things—has too often celebrated its own (dis)interested attitude towards the facts being accumulated. These divergent tendencies—of an ahistorical naïveté that "forgets" the past and of an apolitical disinterestedness that naturalizes sexual difference in terms of a politics of subordination—are both addressed, directly, by the text and circumstances of *The Woman As Good as the Man.* So let us focus on the congruity of historical and political interests by noticing the textual "fact" of the publication, in 1677, of an English translation of the Frenchman's text.

The appearance of "A. L."'s translation seems not to have been one of the crucially important literary events in England that year. Indeed, the first direct evidence of *The Woman's* influence in England appears more than sixty years later, in 1739, with the publication of the celebrated "Sophia" pamphlets. But this evidence is divided against itself since, in affirming the persistence of Poullain's ideas, it also indicates the extent to which they had been forgotten or repressed.[26]

The first of the Sophia pamphlets—*Woman Not Inferior to Man: Or, A short and modest Vindication of the natural Right of the Fair-Sex to a perfect Equality of Power, Dignity, and Esteem, with the Men*—appeared in response to a lead article attacking women's rights printed in *Common Sense: Or, The Englishman's Journal* for September 1. Published between 1737 and 1739 by Lyttelton and Chesterfield, *Common Sense* offered a varied fare of political news and social commentary. The offending article begins, "Having lately dip'd into the Works of Monsieur *Tourreil,*[27] a *French* writer of great Reputation, and meeting with something which concerns the Ladies, I shall lay aside Politicks in order to give the Publick a curious Dissertation of this Author, wherein he examines whether it was wisely done to abolish that Law of the *Romans,* by which Women were kept under the Power of Guardians all the Days of their Lives."[28] We recognize at once the witty tone that Rae Blanchard has identified as belonging to one of three distinct groups of writers interested in women at this period. In between the *conservatives,* who display no respect for women as "self-directing individual[s]," and the *reformers,* who were "attempting to bring about social conditions rising above custom and conformable to reason," were the *wits.*[29] These were "chiefly men of letters from whose pens came the literature of 'wit and gallantry,' [who] toyed half-gallantly, half-scornfully, in poetry and essay, with ideas concerning women" (p. 325). The stylistic symptoms in the *Common Sense* piece are obvious enough: the *sprezzatura* of *dip'd into,* the fashionable acquaintance with French writers, and the casual condescension of "laying aside" the important questions of politics for those concerning ladies. But this piece of gallantry did publicly offer the occasion for a serious reply in the rationalistic and critical style of the reformer.

Published later that year, *Woman Not Inferior* quotes passages from the *Common Sense* piece in order to analyze, and thereby refute, their absurdity.[30] In addition to this critique, however, Sophia also makes substantial arguments on behalf of women's equality that, according to C. A. Moore in 1916, make Mary Wollstonecraft seem "meek and old fashioned."[31] Moore goes on, however, to conclude that Sophia "was a rank imposter" who "perpetrated one of the cleverest hoaxes of her time," by demonstrating that whoever "Sophia" may have been,[32] *Woman Not Inferior* "did little more than adapt François Poullain's 'De l'Égalité des deux Sexes'"

(p. 195). The indignation is historically unjustifiable and rather beside the point, though, since originality was still of rather dubious value then, and authorship never quite signified ownership in the way it has come to do in our age of copyright. Transcribing large sections of another's argument —most of Part 1 of *The Woman* and sections of Part 2 appear wholesale in *Woman Not Inferior*—and not acknowledging one's sources had a venerable tradition in the transmission of philosophical texts during the Renaissance. Nor, in 1739, did the silent rewriting of Poullain's text stop here. As Moore noticed, the second pamphlet in the series, entitled *Man Superior to Woman: Or, A Vindication of Man's Natural Right of Soveraign Authority Over the Woman,* also borrows from Poullain's work. Ostensibly attacking Sophia's argument, this excessively condescending piece also makes unacknowledged use of material from *The Woman.*[33] But since it does so without taking the opportunity of pointing out Sophia's debt, we can surely infer that the entire controversy—including the third pamphlet written in defence of women in counter to *Man Superior*[34]—was, indeed, not so much a hoax (as Moore would have it) but an important instance of a form of publishing venture not untypical at the time.[35] Arguing both sides of a question had long been a common pedagogical device in rhetorical training, one that early prowoman writers appropriated for their own purposes. *Man Superior* discredits the very argument it advances by exposing the absurdity, illogicality, and pomposity of the position from which that argument is made. It begins, for instance, by pointing out that the subordination of women in past societies is evidence of the superiority of male reason. But we are not expected to take this seriously since it is advanced in terms that imply its unacceptability: "The little Glimmering of Reason, which Heaven bestowed on them [women] out of Compassion to us, that they might be in some Degree a Sort of rational Amusement to us, was sufficient to convince them of the Justness of their Subjection" (p. 2).

Controversial topics—such as women's equality—were commonly debated publicly behind anonymity and complex publishing bluffs.[36] And in 1739 feminism was evidently focusing a good deal of contentious energy. The status of unmarried daughters, which *Common Sense* raised, was addressed—with a plea for their reemployment in jobs that men had taken from them—by "a Lady" in "A new Method for making Women as useful and as capable of maintaining themselves, as the Men are" published in *Gentleman's Magazine* of October. During 1739 Mary Collier emerged from her working-class obscurity to publish *The Woman's Labour* "in angry response" to Stephen Duck's *The Thresher's Labour* (1736), which had trivialized the work done by women in rural communities.[37] At the other end of the social scale, Lady Mary Wortley Montagu had, some months previously, declared for the rights of, if not all women, then at least those who could afford to live unconventionally.[38] In the midst of this debate, largely concerning—as so often in feminist debates under capitalism—women's freedom to enter the workplace on equal terms with men, someone obviously thought about the arguments advanced by Poullain half a century before, and set about orchestrating the appearance of the Sophia pamphlets in order to re-present them to English readers. Evidently, the Frenchman's critique of customary prejudice regarding women was known in England, if only by the author(s) of the Sophia pamphlets. But their silence over the considerable debt to Poullain throughout the controversy suggests that those responsible for the production of these works presumed a readership insufficiently familiar with the Frenchman's work to notice or too indifferent to care. And between 1739 and 1677, no one in England seems to have been sufficiently impressed or influenced by *The Woman As Good as the Man* to have left any records behind.[39] But we should not underestimate the evidence of the Sophia pamphlets: Poullain's ideas were alive and well in England during the early part of the eighteenth century. And they were evidently considered important by those who engineered their reappearance.

It is likely that the threat of war with Spain in 1739, which also threatened to withdraw young men from the labor force and marriage market, may have helped stimulate the feminist discourse of that year.[40] No such immediate controversy occasioned the publication of *The Woman* in 1677, though all the general terms of the debate—especially the legal status of women to hold professional and political office —must have seemed peculiarly resonant in the year when Mary, daughter of the king's brother, married the Protestant prince, William of Orange. Nathaniel Brooks, the publisher of *The Woman,* no doubt considered readers' interests, preoccupations, and expectations when deciding to publish the book. Its packaging is provocatively discreet on the matter of its French origins. Poullain's name does not appear anywhere, not even in the translator's preface dedicated to "the Unprejudiced Reader." Evidently the book was not considered likely to sell by reason of its author's prior reputation. But Brooks must nevertheless have considered it capable of attracting a certain market. Casual browsers among his titles in 1677 would doubtless have reacted in different ways. Some might have responded to the title page announcement "Written Originally in *French,* And Translated into *English* by A. L.," with feelings similar to those that greet the appearance of a new translation into English of a text by a Barthes, a Derrida, or a Kristeva in the London—or New York—of our own times. Some, no doubt, would have put the book down with no more ado. But others would no doubt have felt excited; French ideas were fashionable then, as now.[41] London publishers brought out five translations of works by Descartes between 1649 and 1699 and no fewer than six editions of the same philosopher's works in Latin between 1664 and 1685.[42] Here we might also notice that three English versions of Jacques Du Bosc's *L'Honneste Femme* appeared in London editions between 1639 and 1692,[43] while *The Gallery of Heroick Women* (1652), translated from *La Gallerie des Femmes fortes* (1647) of Pierre Le Moyne by no less a figure than the Marquesse of Winchester, inspired Nahum Tate's *A Present For the Ladies: Being a Historical Vindication of the Female Sex* (1692). But it was not, of course, only French books and ideas that were fashionable. In dedicating her tragedy *The Revolution of Sweden* (1706) to Lady Harriet Godolphin, Catherine Trotter Cockburn writes that, "some greater Geniuses among us [might be incited] to exert themselves and change our Emulation of a Neighbouring Nation's Fopperies, to the commendable Ambition of Rivalling them in their illustrious Women; Numbers we know among them, have made a considerable Progress in the most difficult Sciences, several have gain'd the Prizes of Poesie from their Academies, and some have been chosen Members of their Societies. This without doubt is not from any Superiority of their Genius to ours; But from the much greater Encouragement they receive, by the Public Esteem, and the Honours that are done them" (Sigs. A2–A2ᵛ).⁴⁴ Since Pepys, that avid reader, bibliophile, and man of fashion had stopped writing his *Diary* in 1669, we have no idea whether he ever saw *The Woman,* but we can assume that he—and readers like him—might have shown more than a passing interest in the book because of its French origins.

Several English translations of French texts were published during 1677, suggesting their marketability that year.⁴⁵ But French texts also enjoyed a general notoriety in England after the Restoration. In the opening of Wycherley's *The Country Wife* (1672/74), Horner reports on his return from France: "I have brought over not so much as a Bawdy Picture, no new Postures, nor the second part of the *Ecole des Filles*" (act 1, sc. 1, lines 87–88).⁴⁶ Pepys's experiences with this celebrated text began with a significant cultural misapprehension some years before, in January 1668: "13. Thence homeward by coach and stopped at Martins my bookseller, where I saw the French book which I did think to have for my wife to translate, called *L'escolle de Filles;* but when I came to look into it, it is the most bawdy, lewd book that ever I saw, rather worse than *putana errante*—so that I was ashamed of reading in it."⁴⁷

That Pepys's had imagined *L'École des filles* (1655) would be a useful and instructive exercise for his wife to translate makes his own naïveté and subsequent onanistic relationship with the book all the more intriguing.⁴⁸ (He may, of course, have had Molière's play—*L'École des femmes*—in mind.) Yet, however we read Pepys's misunderstanding of this text's reputation, the incident does suggest a distinct predisposition—on Pepys's part, at least—to take seriously what the French had to say on the subject of women. We can feel pretty certain that if Pepys did see *The Woman* in 1677, he would not have been alone in looking twice at a plainly packaged translation from an anonymous French author.

Nevertheless, English readers in 1677 seem to have accorded "A. L."'s translation a reception similar to the one which had greeted the appearance of the original in Paris four years earlier: indifference.[49] We might have expected Anne Conway and Henry More to have mentioned reading *The Woman* or *De l'égalité*. They had, after all, been engaged in a learned correspondence for over twenty years on the philosophy of Descartes, and *The Woman* is, among other things, a brilliant demonstration of Cartesian method that argues how our notion of *woman* is a cultural construct rather than a natural or biological fact.[50] As Hilda Smith suggests, Poullain used the status of women "as an excellent test case for Descartes' method because it was so clearly a product of traditional and irrational values" (pp. 116–17).[51] Perhaps it was the audacity of Poullain's thesis—which even leads him to advocate that women be allowed to preach, an outrageously "radical" idea in England after 1660—that deterred English readers.[52] Certainly those hoping they had stumbled upon a piece of pornography or even gallantry would soon have been disappointed. On the first page of printed text, the English reader would have been warned against judging a book by its title: "There is nothing more nice and delicate, than to Treat on the Subject of *Women*. When a Man speaketh to their advantage, it is presently imagined a peece of Gallantry, or Love: And it is very probable, that the most part Judging of this discourse by the Title, will take it at first for an effect of the one or the other; and will be glad to know the truth of the motive and designe thereof. Take it thus:" (p. 55). The repartee of that imperative might have encouraged those with a taste for witty exchanges and false defences of women to continue reading, but those who began randomly leafing forward would have quickly discovered that there was no "Gallantry, or Love."

Yet these very themes were among the central preoccupations of high literary culture in the England of 1677 if we can judge from the plays either performed or published this year. Nathaniel Lee's *The Rival Queens,* which opened on 17 March, was such a notable box-office success that it encouraged John Banks's *The Rival Kings.*[53] Dryden's *Tyrannick Love* (1670) was reprinted. His opera *The State of Innocence* (written in 1674), based on *Paradise Lost,* was published, and performances of his *All For Love* ousted Sedley's *Antony and Cleopatra* which had opened at a rival theatre in February.[54] Evidently, the various permutations of the compelling psychodrama of war, women, and power preoccupied the literate and cultivated Londoners of 1677. And this is hardly surprising. In a year when the *London Gazette* reported twice a week on the (not always successful) exploits of the protestant prince destined to win an English princess, how could the cultured and socially aware not be sensitively receptive to the sexual politics of heroic drama?[55] Sedley's Agrippa sounds the topical note in the opening moments of *Antony and Cleopatra* with an address to Caesar:

> Remember, Sir, the joy the World exprest,
> When threatning Wars and Mischiefs you redrest
> With a late Peace, which an Alliance ty'd,
> And your fair Sister made *Antonius* Bride.
> The like again you to the World may give,
> If you content with half of it can live.
>   (Act 1, sc. 1, lines 18–23)[56]

Dividing the nation in two: that, of course, was precisely what Shaftesbury and the emergent "Whig" party were trying to do at the time. While Titus Oates was scurrying about disseminating lies or disinformation in preparation for the Popish Plot of the next year, Shaftesbury was busily discrediting Danby and engineering the strong (Protestant) opposition that would eventually topple (Catholic) James in favor of Prince William in 1688.[57] But in 1677, Sedley's lines would have reminded readers/auditors of Charles's treaty with the Dutch in 1674, and focused attention on the possibility of a marriage alliance.[58]

These plays of 1677 are uniformly reactionary in their representations of female power as an erotic psychodrama of self-destruction. Roxana, one of Lee's rival queens, sounds the Senecan keynote of psychomachic rage that tears her apart:

> Fury, revenge, disdain, and indignation
> Tear my swoln breast, make way for fire and tempest.
> My brain is burst, debate and reason quench'd,
> The storm is up, and my hot bleeding heart
> Splits with the rack, while passions like the winds
> Rise up to Heav'n and put out all the Stars.
> (Act 3, sc.1, lines 52–57)[59]

Rebecca Marshall, who opened in the part of Roxana, made her stage career creating such fiery roles. But a report of Elizabeth Barry's performance of this speech in a revival of the play is telling, since it indicates the studied fascination with which such scenes of female self-destruction were received: "I have heard this Speech spoken in a Rage that run the Actor out of Breath; but Mrs. *Barry* when she talked of *hot bleeding Heart,* seemed to feel a Fever within, which by *Debate* and *Reason* she would *quench.* This was not done with a ranting Air, but as if she were struggling with her Passions, and trying to get the Mastery of them; a peculiar *Smile* she had, which made her look the most genteely malicious Person that can be imagined.[60]

Male-dominated cultures—then as now—are fascinated by the evident fact of exceptional women who cannot help but rise to positions of public, social, and political importance. Such cultures constantly problematize that fascination by representing the spectacle of violence which necessarily destroys those women—their reputations if not their minds and bodies—in one of those reversals that confirm the masculinist status quo ante. We need but consider Aphra Behn, staunch supporter of Charles and aristocratic values, who may have been responsible for as many as three plays produced in 1677. *The Debauchee* in February and *The Counterfeit Bridegroom,* which opened in September have been attributed to her, but *The Rover,* which opened in March, is certainly hers.[61]

The Rover forcefully evokes the civil-war years, when different classes of English women gained significant ground in the battle for social and sexual independence. *The Rover* takes place in Naples where that major political concern of 1677—Catholicism[62]—is explored in the familiar surroundings of love, sex, marriage, and the constant threat of war when young men parade about in dashing uniforms and all are eager to love since today may prove their last chance. Lest we forget that Angellica, the courtesan, is not only a professional but a papist to boot, we are reminded of the fact in the climactic scene in which, pistol to her lover's breast, she delays pulling the trigger. "Yet," she trembles ("*pausingly,*" as the stage direction suggests), "I would give thee—time for—penitence." Willmore, English and cavalier to the end, meets this respite in her hysterical, murderous rage with a casual "Faith Child, I thank God, I have ever took Care to lead a good sober, hopeful Life, and am of a Religion That teaches me to believe, I shall depart in peace" (act 5, sc. 1, lines 236–42).[63]

By representing these familiar themes of love and death, religion and politics, the courtly dramas of 1677 reaffirmed London audiences' expectations that to be human was to experience inner conflict. "For in our Playes," Lee writes in dedicating *The Rival Queens* to Lady Katherine Herbert, "you read your own Characters, and they are at best what we have gathered from you" (Sig. A3ᵛ). Unless we ourselves resemble the site of emotional contradictions such as those rending apart the exceptionally powerful women of these plays, our identity as "fully human" individuals is itself somehow in question. The ideological fix, though, is emphatically masculine. This is especially true in Behn's *The Rover*, where Willmore "chooses" Hellena not so much out of any natural predisposition on his part to perceive her obvious virtues but precisely because she takes it upon herself to make them conspicuously apparent to him. Behn distinguishes nicely between Angellica's professional self-advertisement and Hellena's rather desperate resolve "to provide" herself with "a handsome proper fellow" (act 1, sc. 1, lines 38–39) that will rescue her from the confinement of the nunnery and the unwelcome advances of "my lady abbess" (act 3, sc. 1, line 42). By thus representing the dilemma of the exceptional woman in this composite portrayal of contending heterosexual characters, Behn achieves a formally neat resolution by which the professional woman loses ground against an adversary who more closely resembles the dutiful, though "equal," wife.[64]

Equal but subordinate: "this was doctrine to appeal to moderate constitutionalists as patriarchalism seemed to go with the Divine Right of Kings."[65] Protestant "feminism" had entertained only the paradoxical equality of women as household companions; but that would have been no small achievement since it would necessitate nothing less than a restructuring of the inner life.[66] By 1677 it seems that English readers were developing psychological problems that, even though gender definitions then were so different from ours, remain startlingly recognizable today. For several generations, the English people had been re-formed according to social and gender codes based on Reformation theology.[67] Milton's Adam and Eve are familiar models.[68] And there seems to be general reason to think that English readers in 1677 were preoccupied by feelings and psychological concerns not dissimilar to ours. They sought professional help for familiar problems. The records of the astrologer Richard Napier show that between 1597 and 1634 upwardly mobile people of all social groups sought expert advice for emotional problems in gender-specific ways. Both men and women, apparently, were mostly affected by emotional questions concerning personal relationships with members of the immediate family. But men, who formed the significant minority of Napier's clients, were far more likely to be concerned with financial worries than women were.[69] In the years before the civil wars, the anxieties peculiar to a capitalist economy were already shaping a relatively autonomous gender ideology familiar to English readers from Reformation theology.[70]

The sensational divorces of Henry VIII stimulated a mid-sixteenth-century interest in one of the more durable debates in western cultures—the contradiction in marriage between personal affection and social function. How *do* love and marriage go together?[71] The king had made his views perfectly clear in defiance of papal and traditional authority: a Protestant male marries to produce heirs. Her father's paranoid concern over his inability to produce a male heir no doubt contributed to Elizabeth's decision to remain unwed. But Henry had special problems: there was nothing reformist or peculiarly Protestant about patrilinear inheritance. The reformist debate over marriage in the middle decades of the sixteenth century produced an important printed discourse that systematically refocuses, for re-forming readers, the general aristocratic admiration for women so long as they rule in the domestic setting only. An early example, Edmund Tilney's *A brief and pleasant discourse of duties in Mariage; called the Flower of Frendshippe* of 1568, has been noted as being, like Poullain's work, ahead of its times for directly considering the possibility of equality in marriage.[72] *Friendship* is the keyword of the title, signaling the emergent belief among male writers in productive companionship within the married state. Tilney's delightful black-letter fantasy details the mutual duties of husbands and wives since, without agreement on certain important questions such as male authority, the family will not function as efficiently as it might.[73] The double standard over sexual licence, which women writers such as Christine de Pisan (1364–1430?) had attacked long ago, is vehemently attacked here not because it imposes an unjustly differential restraint upon female sexuality, but because it so directly endangers a stable system of claims to property (Sig. B7ᵛ–B8ᵛ).[74] The argument is couched throughout in emotional terms of personal affection that seek to constrain women's sexual activity.[75] Since women are presumed to be continually both sexually available and subject to illicit male desire—"if she once fasten her eyes on a nother, he shall enioy her in spite of hir husbands beard" (Sig. B6)—husbands are encouraged to keep themselves at the center of their wives' affections. "The man," readers are informed, "that is not lyked, and loved of his mate, holdeth his lyfe in continuall perill, his goodes in great ieopardies, his good name in suspect, and his whole house in utter perdition" (Sig. B6). If people needed to be told to love their spouses under threat of "continuall perill," then we can only assume that they all too often didn't. Affectionate marriage could offer women freedom from—or comfort while still under—the stern law of the father.[76] Unfortunately, affection seems often to have led to the tyranny of the husband. If Behn offers any advice to women 'n *The Rover,* it is merely to reaffirm the bind: keep your virginity and use your wit to trap a man whom you can see through and, consequently, hope to manage.

If we are to understand fully just how revolutionary the critique of masculine ideology offered by *The Woman As Good as the Man* really is, then, it is important that we understand why it was that Poullain's ideas had so little apparent effect upon English readers in 1677.[77] For we can recognize in that lack of receptivity an all-too-familiar condition of false consciousness, an ideological blindness to *this* because of a culturally encoded preoccupation with *that.* To continue with Behn's *The Rover* as symptomatic, the *that* was often the civil war, a period in recent and remembered history that could be easily and powerfully evoked by the swashbuckling male heroes and women relatively free from the familiar constraints of a stable society. For audiences in 1677, the living memory of the civil wars must have provided a predisposition to feel, with extraordinary sensitivity, the divisions and tensions associated with what we call class and gender. During the revolutionary decades women assumed unprecedented personal freedoms and degrees of social responsibility. Women from the poorer classes were crucial in organizing some of the more radical sectarian movements of the 1640s. In 1641, the Independent Katherine Chidley founded a church at Bury St. Edmunds that was still active in 1648.[78] Daughters and wives of all classes became accustomed to controlling their households in the absence of men. But with the Restoration of the Stuarts in 1660, all that changed. The men returned to put women back into their traditional places.[79] Behn's complicity in the traditional ideology—her spectacle of the powerful woman finally being put out of business and her valorization of chaste domesticity—comes wrapped up in a countermemory that encourages us to forget just how much women had once achieved. Her treatment of fraternal bonding and rape in *The Rover* is a different matter; on the horrors of masculinist sexuality Behn is both acute and accurate. But her commitment to a dynastic politics that centers freedom for women exclusively on marriage is mystified by the romantic charm of a recent war. The play too conveniently forgets the de facto social achievements of English women during the social instability of the 1640s and 1650s when sectarian women developed a theory and a practice of social equality. Besides demanding self-governance, the right to speak and to share in the running of the congregation, Independent and Brownist women assumed a control over—and freedom within—the marriage contract such as they had not enjoyed previously (except perhaps in theory).

The dominantly masculinist ideology unreceptive to *The Woman* in 1677 replaced the memory of these women with the fantasy of romantic love leading to marriage. The sectarian women were submitted to systematic satire, in part because they threatened the traditional power of husbands. As Thomas writes, "with the sectarian women . . . were popularly associated advanced views on marriage and divorce.

We will not be wives
And tie up our lives
    To villainous slavery."[80]

Although Reformation ideology was bound to a doctrine of spiritual equality between the sexes, in England it tended to cancel out the radical implications in a typically patriarchal way by a division of social function that effectively depoliticized women's power into the familiar public/private dichotomy. Women's souls were equal and free, and women deserved to be treated as equal within marriage in accordance with the respect due to their responsibilities helping to manage the family property.[81] But here their social power stops. In 1641 Katherine Chidley, the "most militant of [the] feminine pamphleteers," still announced the husband's right "over her in bodily and civil respects, but not," she insists, "to be a lord over her conscience."[82] In general, it was this dominant separation of women's rights from broader social and political questions that the sectarian women threatened during the civil war when they stepped outside the privacy of marriage onto the public stage of civil affairs.

Back in 1568, Tilney's courtly chat on marital friendship had brought Vives and Erasmus together in a debate that celebrates women's equality within marriage (Sig. D8). Yet this debate ends by insisting that ultimate authority resides with the husband. For a tricky situation, such as an adulterous husband, the tale is told of how a model wife gently shames her husband into loving her the more by acting in a friendly, rather than scornful, way. In this story the wife—pretending to be her husband's sister—visits the (lower-class) girl and, in a friendly manner, provides her with "a good bed, well furnished, and hangings, with other necessaries" (Sig. E5^v) more suited to the man's social status. On his next clandestine visit the husband, humbled and humiliated at this testimony of his wife's devotion, realizes that he loves her all the more. Meanwhile, the possible friendship between the women—already undermined by the wife's initial deception—is denied since it would too directly threaten the heterosexual monogamy central to property rights.[83] The folkloric elements of the story are fascinating: that bed, which serves as talismanic and fetishized gift, at once testifies to the wife's real (material) social control (the ability to give away something belonging to her family) at the same time that it redirects the husband's desire for the (class-) other into an intensified desire for the (legitimate-) same. Although it seems to be offering a model for wifely behavior, the tale better serves as an instance of what we have come to recognize as commodity fetishism.[84]

By 1677 the Reformation commitment to women's equality seems not to have advanced beyond spiritual freedom in England. Yet in recognizing the important assault on the sexual double standard waged in some Reformation texts on marriage,[85] we should not underestimate the importance of freedom of conscience any more than the very real constraints maintained on women politically. As in Tilney, marital equality remains an ideal of domestic organization directed towards the maintenance of household goods, the familiar bourgeois pattern. After examining the English books of advice on marriage published between the mid-sixteenth and mid-seventeenth centuries, Wright concludes that "despite the ubiquitous nature of such counsel, the demand increased for books devoted exclusively to family affairs" (p. 215). "There is," he adds, "a strange sameness in point of view and treatment in the books read by the burgher of 1558 and by his grandson in 1640" (p. 226). Surely, then, we need to infer that this increasing need for books that offered the same advice indicates not only a growing number of married persons aspiring to the ideal being offered but also that more people felt that they needed expert advice on predictable problems affecting their married lives. As Kathleen Davies suggests, the popularity of conduct manuals on marriage "may have had more to do with a taste familiar among modern middle-class readers for reading descriptions of their own life-style" (p. 578). Far from solving the problems of family life, the advice being directly and implicitly offered may have served to perpetuate those very ideas, opinions, expectations, and values that were causing the problems in the first place.[86]

Structurally, the marital ideal of affectionate domesticity seems to have been invariably under strain right from the start; hence the increasing need for more of the same advice on the same problems from the experts who write books. At least the ideal proved unable to resolve the conflicting demands which it imposed—of mutual affection, security and prosperity—since it is based upon the subordination of women and the exploitation of their labor. The latter topic, we've seen, focused attention in 1739 and remains a problem today. In 1677, *The Woman* did not advance a fully nuanced critique of the bourgeois family, but it did—and still does—offer the basis for a much broader feminist critique of the gender biases fundamental to modern European and American culture. It exposes as ideological those sociosexual relationships that continue to exploit women in general and wives in particular. Once we have accepted Poullain's Cartesian premise—that many of our ideas of things are culturally predetermined for us—we can recognize that only cultural presuppositions limit our concept of woman. There are, then, only man-made reasons for women not taking a full and equal part in the social and political life outside of the "private" space of marriage and domestic organization. Since culture, being neither natural or divine, is reversible, there is no reason not to think about allowing women to preach, and to train for and hold medical, legal, and political office. Poullain does not suggest how an egalitarian society is to be brought about, but he does open up the necessary critique of early modern bourgeois society by arguing, in a rational manner, for women's social freedom and political equality.

Since members of those cultures that speak, read, and write English today still commonly confuse what is "natural" with what is "cultural"—especially with regard to the politics of women's subjectivity—we can hardly be surprised that English readers took little notice of *The Woman* when it appeared three hundred years ago. There was little enough room for such a text in Restoration culture with its drives to erase the past of sectarian liberation. The official culture of court and stage offered a staple diet of modern ideology: the exceptional woman, however socially powerful, is a sex object rather than a social subject. In those great plays of 1677, actresses such as Elizabeth Barry, Mrs. Betterton, Anne

Hughes, and Rebecca Marshall portrayed female characters whose social independence and even political eminence necessarily preceded either the spectacular erotosadism of self-destruction or the minatory acceptance of social control in the form of a romantic (though often elaborately and explicitly contractual) marriage. Spiced up with innuendo directed at contemporary scandals and topical debates, these plays helped confirm masculinist norms in the process of celebrating the erotic friction generated by those women who rose to challenge them.

The romance of military heroism came to an unanticipated climax in October with the marriage of William and Mary. Publicly announced on the twenty-second,[87] it was recorded by Ralph Josselin, the vicar of Earls Colne in Essex, on the twenty-eighth: "Oct. 28. dewing. the news of the Ladie Marias marrying the prince of Orange pleased the Kingdom, god good to us in many mercies." But less than a month later, Josselin demonstrates the wariness of one shrewdly experienced in political matters: "Nov. 16. Heard that the city was alarmed that the papists plotted a massacre there, was the marriage a pillow to lull us asleepe."[88] Having lived through the civil wars, himself a nonconformist minister with all the aspirations and insecurities of the petit bourgeoisie, Josselin obviously brings a highly personal sensibility to bear upon the events. Still, if he understood that public events, like royal marriages, often distract us from what is *really* going on —different from the fantasy dreamed while we succumb to the lulling effect of that pillow—then he might have understood the premises of the critique of masculinist ideology offered in *The Woman*.

But Josselin leaves no record of having encountered Poullain's ideas and is doubtless more typical of English readers of the 1670s and 1680s in that than in his imaginative grasp of how official culture works. That he and others ignored *The Woman* is no reason, however, for us to do so. Rather, it might suggest that the history of the ignored or forgotten Frenchman and his ideas is a typical forgetting of the arguments for women's equality, in which "English" culture of our times continues to participate. If the critique we find in *The Woman* of the cultural construction of *woman* as a social subject still hasn't been allowed to catch on, we need only consider recent studies of representations of women in pornography, modern advertising, popular films, and popular romances to begin understanding how and why this has happened. The evolutionary forces of Reformation ideology and the market economy that had been transforming English society for several generations by 1677 have persistently identified themselves with traditional values based on male supremacy and the accumulation of private property.

In the historical era we share with Poullain, "A. L.," Nathaniel Brooks, Pepys, Aphra Behn, Elizabeth Barry, Ralph Josselin, and English readers of 1677, that masculinist ideology continues to dominate bourgeois life by, inter alia, enforcing a gender system that subordinates women to the limited (or false) freedoms of selfhood in subordination, especially within marriage. To quote from Louis B. Wright again, "If in general . . . the guides to domestic felicity reiterated for decade after decade the same counsel, *it merely* indicates the fundamental quality of much of the advice, which *to this day remains valid* in bourgeois society" (p. 227, emphasis added). As cultural historians, we need Poullain and *The Woman* in order to avoid this kind of opacity, lest cultural history itself remain an ideology and not a practice. There is clearly something very wrong with a society that still needs the same advice on very basic questions of family life after three hundred years. If not for decades and decades but for centuries, readers of English have learned to consume romances and practical guides to marriage and family life, then it may be time to stop forgetting Poullain. We need cultural history to understand and control the world around us; not only so we can see how we arrived at our present state but so that we can think through the possibilities of alternate directions our culture hasn't yet taken. And we should not forget the sectarian women whose real social advances Poullain's theory would have supported. *The Woman,* which appeared during the crucial early development of the modern era, may help us understand how we got here so that we might better see our way out of our persistent problems, which mark a social and cultural impasse.

Notes

1. Beauvoir, *Second Sex,* p. 107.

2. Stock, "Poullain de La Barre"; Magné, "Le féminisme de Poullain de La Barre"; Alcover, *Poullain de La Barre;* and the articles by Elisabeth Badinter, Daniel Armogathe, Geneviève Fraisse, and Christine Fauré in *Corpus* 1 (1985): 13–49 listed separately in the Works Cited. There is some uncertainty regarding the spelling of our author's name stemming, in part, from his own willingness to spell it both *Poulain* and *Poullain;* see Alcover (pp. 9–10).

3. *De l'égalité* was licensed on 23 July. A pirated edition appeared in Lyons the same year. A second printing appeared in 1676, again by DuPuis and again a pirated edition appeared in Lyons set from the previous Lyons edition. A "Seconde Edition" of 1679 is a reissue of the 1676 edition with a new title page. In 1690, a pirated edition appeared in Geneva with a false title page reading "A Paris." Another issue of this appeared in 1692. For a thorough bibliographical description of these works and the various piratings and reissues, see Alcover, *Poullain de La Barre,* pp. 21–30, and Daniel Armogathe, "De l'égalité des deux sexes," who mentions a 1691 edition (p. 26, n. 16). For *De l'excellence,* see Alcover, *Poullain de La Barre,* pp. 12–15. In "Autour du mythe de la femme," François Moureau discusses an unpublished refutation of *De l'égalité* entitled "Supériorité de l'homme sur la femme ou l'inégalité des deux sexes dédiée à Jèsus-Christ." An earlier book from this period has also been attributed to Poullain, *Les Rapports de la langue Latine avec la Françoise.*

4. I am grateful to Felicity Nussbaum for suggesting these names; both appear in Patricia Crawford's "Womens' Published Writings 1600–1700." I have not systematically checked for authors signing themselves "L. A.," a useful suggestion made by Moira Ferguson.

5. See Levingston, *State of the Case in brief,* November 1654, and *A true Narrative of the Case* (1655).

6. The play was published by J. Magres and R. Bently, the romance by Robert Sollers. Other works of La Roche-Guilhem's that appeared at around the same time include the *Journal Amoureux d'Espagne* printed in the Netherlands under the fictitious imprint "Corneille Egmon: Cologne" in 1675. Two editions—in French—of her novel *Almanzaïde* appeared in 1676; Magres and Bently published an English translation—by an unknown hand—under the title *Almanzor and Almazida* in 1678.

7. An English translation appeared under the title *The History of Female Favourites* in 1772. Neither the Dublin edition of J. Exshow or the London edition of C. Parker identifies the translator.

8. A "Second Edition" (London: Abel Swalle, 1688) of this translation in the British Library (shelfmark 1477.dd.60), not listed in Wing, *Short-Title Catalogue,* or by F. F. Madan in his essay *Milton, Salmasius, and Dugard* which examines sixteen printings of Bate's *Elenchus,* is—presumably—a reissue of the 1685 edition with a new title page.

9. À Wood, *Athenae Oxonienses* 2:304. The works in question, presumably, are the translations of Maimbourg and Simon.

10. Venn and Venn, *Alumni Cantabrigienses,* pt. 1.

11. His name, at least, does not appear in Collins, *Registers and Monumental Inscriptions.*

12. For further details concerning the controversy over Burnet's *Theory,* see Basil Willey, Introduction to *Theory of the Earth;* idem, *Eighteenth-Century Background,* pp. 27–35, 37, 41; and Marjorie Hope Nicolson, *Mountain Gloom and Mountain Glory,* chap. 6. My account here is also indebted to Leslie Stephen's entry for *Burnet* in the *Dictionary of National Biography.* In *The Providence of Wit,* Martin Battestin offers some engaging readings of Burnet's *Theory* (see especially pp. 35–38, 41, 46, 49, 134–35, 146, 296–97).

13. Samuel Hearne, *Domus Carthusiana,* p. 181.

14. The *Reflections* is actually signed "A. L." but has been attributed to Lovell in the library user's catalogue (but not the published *General Catalogue)* of the British Library, which seems a reasonable attribution, given the publisher.

15. Lovell also translated Cyrano de Bergerac's *The Comical History of the States and Empires of the Worlds of the Moon and Sun* (London: Henry Rhodes, 1687), Antoine Gombaud Méré's *Conversations of the Mareschal of Clerambault and the Chevalier de Méré* (London: Henry Brome, 1677), and Louis Maimbourg's *An Historical Treatise Of The Foundation and Prerogatives of the Church of Rome* (London: James Hindemarsh, 1685).

16. *The British Library General Catalogue of Printed Books to 1975,* 360 vols. (London: Bingley and Saur, 1979–1987), 201:275.

17. See Pope, *Rape of the Lock,* p. 356.

18. In "The Translator's Advice to the Reader," "A. L." expresses understandable pique that another translation, by Philip Ayres, had already appeared. But Ayres, according to "A. L.," has turned de Villars into a believer in the Cabalistic and Rosicrucian doctrines with which the romance is concerned. "I confess," "A. L." writes, "my Eyes were not so good, as to discover that dangerous flaw in my *Author* when I set upon the translating of him; for if I had, I should not have been so bold to have attempted it, being conscious of my own inability to encounter the Giants of the *Cabal* with no better Weapon than *Ens Rationis, or Universale a parte rei"* (Sig. A3). *Ens Rationis* is also a tag popular with the translator of *The Woman* (see "Entia Rationis," p. 117).

19. There are seven, two of which purport to be translations from French originals though neither of them is very likely to have been by the same person who translated Poullain. Jean de Bernières Louvigny's *The Interiour Christian: or The interiour conformity; which Christians ought to have with Jesus Christ* (Antwerp [London?], 1684), an enthusiastic piece of evangelical propaganda, is entirely out of keeping with the rationalism of Poullain's argument. The short pamphlet, *A Letter from a French Lawyer* (London: Richard Chiswell, 1689) which attempts to prove that the French will support the Glorious Revolution of William of Orange despite their apparent support for James II, is likely to be not a translation at all but a piece of political propaganda. While it might well be by Lovell, there is no reason to link it with the translator of *De l'egalité.* Three works from the 1640s—one of them in verse—are probably too early to have been by the "A. L." who translated Poullain. *An Inducement to the Intrenching of the City of York* (1642) is one of those polemics in heroic couplets that the first year of the civil war inspired. The other two works by

"A. L." are *A true relation of the late expedition of . . . the Earl of Ormond* (London: Joseph Hunscott, 1642), which claims to have been written by a commander in the army, and *To all the honest, wise and grave citizens of London* (1648). The second is a call for peace that includes disbanding the army. Either could be by Lovell, who might well have spent time in uniform—this would help explain his association with the Charterhouse—but there is nothing in either to help us identify the translator in question. Since the author of *A Question Deeply concerning Married Persons, and such as intend to Marry* published by Thomas Underhill in 1653 declares that he is "aged now 83 years" (p. 7), we can surely assume that this too is not the work of the translator of Poullain who would—by my reckoning—then be 107 years old when *The Woman* appeared. Moreover, *A Question* is a distinctly misogynistic text, employing copious scriptural arguments to deny women the right to own property independently of their fathers or husbands. This is hardly the kind of argument we would expect from the translator of a text on women's equality. Finally, there is no obvious reason to associate the "A. L." who wrote *An Impartial and full Account of the Life and Death of the Unhappy Lord Russel, Eldest Son and Heir of the Present Earl of Bedford, who was Executed for High Treason, July 21, 1683* (London: Caleb Swinock, 1684) with either Lovell or the translator of Poullain de La Barre.

20. For an excellent survey of the impact of scientific thought upon English society at the time, see Michael Hunter's *Science and Society,* which contains a first-rate account of Sprat's *History* (pp. 29–31).

21. This marginal gloss appears on p. 29 of Coleridge's copy of the *Travels* now in the British Library (shelfmark c.126.1.5). Coleridge's comments make fascinating reading. At p. 127, where the text reads "the Port of *Caire,*" he has noted "c'est le mot Français." And on p. 133, where Lovell has written "the figure of a Spit, or a Hebrew Lamed," Coleridge has written "What can this mean?—Rather, how shall I write a Ha! Ha! laugh against myself? Instead of the Hebrew L, I read it a Hebrew lam'd—a lame Jew." He clearly felt so pleased with this witticism that he signed it *S.T.C.* Usually, though, his marginal comments betray his distaste for things French. "Scarce a leaf in this Book, as far as I have read, which has not the word 'Lovely': & 9 times out of 10 misapplied. *Fort aimable.* It is however characteristic of a Frenchman—in all ages a Frenchman Γαλλοι αει Γ'αλλοι!" (p. 113), i.e., "the French are indeed always others" or, in contemporary American, "totally different." My thanks to Martha Malamud and Michael Lane for help unpacking this multilingual pun which depends for its visual effect on Coleridge's (deliberately?) incorrect accenting and capitalization. The phrase should read Γάλλοι ἀεὶ γ'άλλοι.

22. Dryden, Preface to *Ovid's Epistles,* 1:268.

23. Cotgrave, *Dictionarie.*

24. Kelly, "Early Feminist Theory." Ian MacLean's learned *Renaissance Notion of Woman,* for instance, makes no reference to the *querelle* at all. Since the appearance of Kelly's article, important work on the position of women and feminist thought in early modern England has been produced, including Ferguson, *First Feminists;* Nussbaum, *The Brink of All We Hate;* Smith, *Reason's Disciples;* Woodbridge, *Women and the English Renaissance;* and Henderson and McManus, *Half Humankind.*

25. See, for example, Althusser, "Ideology and Ideological State Apparatuses"; Barrett, *Women's Oppression Today;* and especially idem, "Ideology." For a brief account of the importance and intellectual context of Poullain's ideas, see Seidel, "Poullain de La Barre's *The Woman.*"

26. See *Reason's Disciples,* where Hilda Smith notices "strong similarities between [Poullain's] work and the anonymous *[An Essay] In Defence of the Female Sex"* (p. 117) and has suggested that William Walsh "borrowed much from Poullain de La Barre" for his *Dialogue Concerning Women, Being a Defence of the Sex* of 1691 (p. 193). More generally, Smith suggests that Poullain was, like Cornelius Agrippa, a source that "later women feminists drew on" (p. 193). I have, however, been unable to find evidence of specific influence on *An Essay* or Walsh's poem; though it is, perhaps, pertinent here that the third edition of *An Essay* dismisses Walsh as "a false Renegade [who] fights under our Colours only for a fairer Opportunity of betraying us" (p. 4). In *Feminism in Eighteenth-Century England,* Katherine Rogers found nothing to say about Poullain or the influence of his work. Scholars studying the European scene have had more luck. Ellen McNiven Hine's "The Woman Question" shows that Buffier, Marvan de Bellegarde, and Montesquieu all "owed Poullain without acknowledgment," though the English writers Locke and Halifax "owe nothing" (p. 66). More recently, Pauline Kra has written of "feminist theories in the tradition of Poulain de La Barre" (p. 275) in her "Montesquieu and Women."

27. Jacques de Tourreil (1656–1715) devoted much of his life to translating Demosthenes. He was employed by the Academie français on the *Dictionnaire* and was honoured with the privilege of presenting the first copy to the king. See *Nouvelle Biographie Générale,* 45:547–48.

28. *Common Sense,* issue 135.

29. Blanchard, "Richard Steele."

30. On the tradition of prowoman writers who scrutinized and disabled the traditional discourse of misogyny, see Simon Shepherd's informative and lively introduction to his edition of *The Woman's Sharp Revenge: Five Women's Pamphlets from the Renaissance,* pp. 9–23.

31. Moore, "The First of the Militants."

32. One "Medley" suggested Lady Sophia Fermor, "the second wife of Lord Carteret" in "Sophia, A Lady of Quality." Since then no one seems to have discovered positively who Sophia was, if indeed a single person was responsible. While Lady Mary Wortley Montagu's name has often been suggested, she was out of the country at the time. In *First Feminists,* Ferguson reports that Lady Mary's biographer, Robert Halsband, has concluded the evidence to be inconclusive (p. 46).

33. In *The Learned Lady in England,* Myra Reynolds found the piece difficult to assess, but its excessively exaggerated tone and use of innuendo suggest that it is clearly ironical. Indeed, a passage such as the following illustrates how the work aims its satire beyond the confines of women. The target here—Bishop Gilbert Burnet whose *History of His Own Times* began to appear in 1724 (volume 2 appeared in 1734)—was a common butt of Tory satire: "For *History* I think [women] have an uncommon Capacity: At least one of the most noted Productions in that Kind is thought to be the Work of a female Genius. For though a Reverend Bishop, in Compliance with the Modesty of it's real Author, was so kind to lend his Name to the celebrated History of his own Times, it is believed by many that his Chaplain's old Grandmother had the chief Hand in it" (Sophia, *Man Superior to Woman,* p. 50).

34. The three tracts were collected and republished under the title *Beauty's Triumph: Or, The Superiority of the Fair Sex invincibly proved* in 1751, suggesting a contrived three-part debate leading to the final victory of the feminist argument. Felicity Nussbaum (*The Brink of All We Hate,* p. 8) has suggested that the second and

third "Sophia" pamphlets are translations of works by Poullain de La Barre, written subsequently to *De l'égalité,* his *De l'éducation des dames* (1674), and his *De l'-excellence des hommes contre l'égalité des sexes* (1675). See also Nussbaum, *Satires On Women,* p. ix; Ferguson, *First Feminists,* p. 20; and Williamson, Introduction to *Female Poets of Great Britain,* p. xiv.

35. For a contemporary discussion of the reasons for women writers to hide behind anonymity at this time, see the preface to *An Essay In Defence of the Female Sex* (1691), which is partly reprinted in Ferguson, *First Feminists,* pp. 205–8. Besides making the traditional argument that authors should not seek the glory of personal renown, the preface warns women writers to consider "the tenderness of Reputation in our Sex" (Sigs. A7ᵛ–A8) when signing their works. This problem is especially sensitive when women are writing in defence of their own sex since some men "whenever provok'd, especially by a Woman" (Sig. A8) are likely to start a scandal. The *Essay* "Written by a Lady," is probably by Judith Drake; see Ferguson, *First Feminists,* pp. 201–2, and Smith, *Mary Astell,* pp. 173–82.

36. See, for example, the debate over the authority of *An Essay in Defence of the Female Sex* in Ferguson, *First Feminists,* p. 201, and the feminist satire *Mundus Muliebris* (1690), probably by Mary Evelyn, which was answered by *Mundus Foppiensis* (1691). Margaret Hunt's "Hawkers, Bawlers, and Mercuries" provides an excellent survey.

37. The phrase is Ferguson's, who reprints selections from Collier's poem with brief commentary in *First Feminists,* pp. 257–65. Duck's *The Thresher's Labour* and Collier's *The Woman's Labour* were recently reprinted with an introduction by Ferguson.

38. See Ferguson, *First Feminists,* pp. 20–21. Wortley Montagu's *Nonsense of Common Sense* # 6 is dated Tuesday, January 24, 1738.

39. In her *Mary Astell,* Florence Smith remarks that "the English translation . . . does not seem to have been known to Mary Astell" (p. 177). Myra Reynolds observes that *The Woman* "does [not] seem to have been well known in the seventeenth century" before suggesting that it might have been "too radical and uncompromising" for Astell (p. 289).

40. Such, at least, was the immediate occasion offered by the editorial headnote to the article in *Gentleman's Magazine,* which observes: "If the War which is proclaim'd against *Spain* should become general and very destructive, the following Scheme by a Lady, who is a new Correspondent, will probably meet with attention" (*A New Method,* p. 525). A. H. Upham identified the growth of a significant printed discourse regarding feminist topics in England during the last three decades of the seventeenth century in "English *Femmes Savantes,*" adducing the general imitation of the French court, with its emphasis upon women as "shrewd, designing, deceptive and inconstant" (p. 263).

41. This is testified by the appearance in 1677 of a second edition of Pierre Lainé's *The Princely Way to the French Tongue.*

42. See Wing, *Short-title Catalogue.*

43. See: *The Compleat Woman. Written in French by Monsieur Du-Bosc . . . And now faithfully Translated into English, by N.N.* (1639), *The Accomplish'd Woman. Written in FRENCH, since made ENGLISH, By The Honourable Walter Montague. Esq* (1656), and *The Excellent Woman Described by Her True Characteristics and Their Opposites* (1692). This last has often been attributed to Theophilus Dorrington, as has *The Secretary of Ladies. Or, A new collection of letters and an-*

swers composed by Moderne Ladies and Gentlemen (1638) which is also a translation, by Jerome Hainhofer, from Du Bosc. Unlike *The Woman,* these all belong to the humanist tradition of courtesy books that offer advice, warnings, and models of behavior for would-be gentlefolk.

44. I am grateful to Marilyn Williamson for drawing my attention to this passage and to the translations of works by Du Bosc and Le Moyne.

45. Notable translations of La Calprenède's *Pharamond* and Madeleine de Scudéri's *Almahide* by John Phillips appeared in 1677. Some indication of the market for books of French origins can, perhaps, be gauged by an advertisement appearing in Nathaniel Lee's *Rival Queens* of this year. Under the heading "Some Books Printed this Year, 1677, for *J. Magres,* and *R. Bentley,*" it lists twenty titles, eight of which are "*French* Novels." And of the other twelve, two are translations from French, Gabriel de Brémond's "*The Happy Slave,*" and Pierre Nicole's collection of "*Moral Essays*" (Sig. a2ᵛ). In 1677 the same team of Magres and Bentley also produced *The Disorders of Love. Truly expressed In the Unfortunate Amours of Givry Mademoiselle de Guise,* "made *English* from the *French,*" a romance for which a French original probably never existed.

46. Wycherley, *Plays,* p. 241. The play was revived in May 1676, a year before *The Woman* appeared; see the editor's introduction (pp. 241–44) for dates of composition, performance, and publication. On *L'Ecole des filles* (1655), see Foxon, *Libertine Literature in England,* pp. 30–37.

47. Pepys, *Diary,* 9:21–22.

48. See Thompson, *Unfit for Modest Ears,* who supplies the subsequent masturbation sequences (pp. 22–23), and Francis Barker's *Tremulous Private Body,* which develops an elaborate meditation on onanistic reading habits in the early-modern period by starting with Pepys's response to this work. Oddly, Barker quotes from a bowdlerized version of the *Diary,* a strategy that either undermines his own argument or represents a very curious and recondite form of game.

49. "1673. Nanti du privilège royal, *De l'égalité des deux Sexes* parait dans l'indifférence générale" (Elizabeth Badinter, "Ne portons pas," p. 13). But see Alcover, *Poullain de La Barre,* p. 33 and Stock, "Poullain de La Barre," pp. 182–89, who infer from the numerous reprintings over the subsequent thirty years that it must have been reaching a substantial readership. Alcover admits, however, that "le témognages public . . . sont quasi inexistants" (p. 31).

50. Conway, *Conway Letters.*

51. On Cartesian rationalism and feminist discourse in early modern England, see also Perry, "Mary Astell's Response."

52. On the reaction against women preaching and holding church office, see Hill, *World Turned Upside Down,* pp. 250–51; Williams, "Women Preachers"; and Thomas, "Women and the Civil War Sects."

53. On the success of Lee's play and its influence that year on Banks, Dryden, and Samuel Pordage, see Vernon, Introduction to *The Rival Queens,* pp. xiv–xvi.

54. Sedley, *Works,* 1:189–90.

55. See also *Narrative of the Great and Bloody Fight* (1677).

56. Sedley, *Antony and Cleopatra,* pp. 1–2.

57. See Miller, *Popery and Politics,* pp. 121–53.

58. The marriage of William and Mary was rather hastily arranged in October, though the possibility of an alliance between the Stuarts and the House of Orange had been mooted in 1674, the year of the Dutch treaty, when the possibility of

Anne marrying William had been discussed. See Ogg, *England in the Reign of Charles*, p. 384.

59. Lee, *Rival Queens*, p. 26.

60. [Curll], *History of the English Stage*, pp. 19–20.

61. See Goreau, *Reconstructing Aphra*, p. 293. Behn's *Abdelazer; Or, The Moor's Revenge* and *The Town Fopp: Or, Sir Timothy Tawdrey* were also published in 1677.

62. On the increasing pressure for a war against Catholic France early in 1677, see Miller, *Popery and Politics*, p. 148. Central to the anti-Catholic debates of the year was, of course, the problem of Charles's possible—and his brother's definite—Catholicism. In addition to Marvell's *Account of the Growth of Popery*, other notable contributions published in 1677 include Richard Baxter's *Naked Popery* and William Lloyd's *Papists No Catholicks*.

63. Behn, *The Rover*, p. 74.

64. Wifely virtues were also being celebrated in other kinds of writing at the time, including the vast popular literature on courtship. See Spufford, *Small Books*, pp. 129–93, 157, and passim. Readers of the chapbooks Spufford examines would have made unlikely readers of *The Woman*.

65. Hill, *World Turned Upside Down*, p. 248. Mary Astell provides an intriguing counterexample of an early "feminist" who remained committed to absolutism in politics (see Perry, "Mary Astell's Response," p. 14).

66. For the recent debate over the emancipatory possibilities of Protestant ideology, see Woodbridge, *Women and the English Renaissance*, and Lisa Jardine, *Still Harping on Daughters*, pp. 1–8.

67. "The sexual revolution which was an important part of the introduction of the Protestant ethic meant replacing property marriage (with love outside marriage) by a monogamous partnership, ostensibly based on mutual love, and a business partnership in the affairs of the family" (Hill, *World Turned Upside Down*, p. 247). Keith Wrightson emphasizes in detail the class differentials obtaining in the balancing of affection and property (*English Society*, pp. 66–88).

68. See David J. Latt, "Praising Virtuous Ladies," for a useful study of Milton's representation of the first married couple.

69. See MacDonald, *Mystical Bedlam*, pp. 36, 72–111.

70. Chilton L. Powell's *English Domestic Relations* and Louis B. Wright's *Middle-Class Culture* have made us familiar with the emergent patterns of bourgeois ideas of marriage in Elizabethan and early Stuart literature and with the precise reaffirmations of gender roles in the production of social life among literate classes at this time. But see more recent debates on the unreliability of literary evidence when constructing the history of the modern family: Davies, "Sacred Condition of Equality"; Spufford, *Small Books*, pp. 140, 157; Wrightson, *English Society*, pp. 66–118; and Levine, *Family Formation*.

71. For a general survey of the literature on marriage in Renaissance England, see Henderson and McManus, *Half Humankind*, pp. 72–81.

72. See Woodbridge, *Women and the English Renaissance*, p. 60; Hull, *Chaste, Silent, and Obedient*, p. 52; and Dunn, "Changing Image of Woman."

73. See Wrightson, *English Society*, p. 90.

74. See Thomas, "Double Standard," esp. pp. 203–4; and also Hill, who writes "Sexual freedom, in fact, tended to be freedom for men only, so long as there was no effective birth control. This was the practical moral basis to the Puritan em-

phasis on monogamy" (*World Turned Upside Down*, p. 247). Catherine Dunn offers interesting attacks on the double standard in poems by Michael Drayton and Samuel Daniel written during the final years of the sixteenth century in "Changing Image of Woman," pp. 25–26.

75. On the general recognition of women's sexual appetite during the Renaissance, see Henderson and McManus, *Half Humankind*, pp. 55–59. But as David Latt suggests, "For the most part the new acknowledgment of human sexual needs only added to the fear and antagonism male writers felt toward women" ("Praising Virtuous Ladies," p. 57).

76. See Jardine, *Still Harping on Daughters*, pp. 37–67; MacDonald, *Mystical Bedlam*, pp. 72–111; Wrightson, *English Society*, pp. 89–118. Ozment, *When Fathers Ruled*, pp. 50–72 surveys contemporary European attitudes toward the authority of husbands.

77. In *Reason's Disciple's* Hilda Smith writes that seventeenth-century feminist writers generally "were largely forgotten both because the social effect of their thought was limited and because its historical influence was truncated" (p. 192).

78. Williams, "Women Preachers," p. 566. See also Cross, "'He-Goats before the Flocks.'"

79. Hill, *World Turned Upside Down*, p. 306. But see Mary Prior's study, "Women and the Urban Economy," which shows how, for women of upwardly mobile families engaged in business and trade, local market forces and fluctuations in family life brought about by marriage and death could exert as important an influence as larger sociopolitical changes in the nation at large.

80. Thomas, "Women and the Civil War Sects," p. 328.

81. See Rogers, *Matrimoniall Honour*, pp. 236–253 and Latt, "Praising Virtuous Ladies," pp. 41–43.

82. Cited in Thomas, "Women and the Civil War Sects," p. 333. The epithet is from Williams, "Women Preachers," p. 566.

83. As Dr. Johnson commented, it was upon female chastity "that all the property in the world depends" (cited in Thomas, "Double Standard," p. 209). Thomas comments that "fundamentally, female chastity has been seen as a matter of property; not, however, the property of legitimate heirs, but the property of men in women" (pp. 209–210).

84. See Davies, "Sacred Condition of Equality," pp. 568–569 and Thomas, "Double Standard," pp. 207–10.

85. See, for example, Rogers' *Matrimoniall Honour*, chap. 8 (pp. 163–184), "Treating of the 3. Ioint duty of the Marryed, viz. Chastitie" and Thomas, "Double Standard."

86. "Mary of Napier's female patients blamed their own psychological distress on marital problems, and popular works such as the homily on marriage admitted that women suffered from the tribulations of marriage more than men because they relinquished their liberty when they wed" (MacDonald, *Mystical Bedlam*, p. 47).

87. Ogg, *England in the Reign of Charles*, p. 547. The *London Gazette*, 22–25 October 1677 (no. 1245), however, reports the announcement as occurring on the twenty-fourth.

88. Josselin, *Diary*.

The
WOMAN
As GOOD as
the MAN
Or, the Equality
of Both Sexes

Ann Donnellan

R. Southwell

THE
WOMAN
As GOOD as the
MAN:
OR, THE
Equallity of Both *Sexes.*

Written Originally in *French,*
And Translated into *English* by *A. L.*

N B

London: Printed by *T. M.* for *N. Brooks,* at the
Angel in *Cornhil,* 1677.

*Reproduction of the 1677 title page. With
permission of the William Andrews Clark
Memorial Library, University of California,
Los Angeles.*

The Preface,

Containing The Plat-form and Designe, of the Discourse.

*T*HERE is nothing more nice and delicate, than to Treat on the Subject of *Women*.[1] When a Man speaketh to their advantage, it is presently imagined a peece of Gallantry, or Love: And it is very probable, that the most part Judging of this discourse by the Title, will take it at first for an effect of the one or other; and will be glad to know the truth of the motive and designe thereof. Take it thus:

The most happy thought, that can enter into the minds of those who labour, to acquire a solid Science, after that they have been instructed, according to the Vulgar Method, is to doubt if they have been taught aright, and to desire to discover the truth by themselves.

In the progress of their inquiry, it occurs to them necessarily, to observe that we are filled with prejudices, (that is to say, opinions past upon things without true Examination); And that we must absolutely Renounce them, to attain to clear, and distinct Knowledges.

In the designe of insinuating so important a Maxime, we have believed it the best, to choose a determinate, and famous Subject, where every one takes an interest; to the end, that having demonstrated, that a Sentiment as ancient as the World, of as great extent as the Earth, and as Universal as Mankind is a prejudice or errour, the Learned might at length, be Convinced of the necessity of Judging of things by themselves after having examined them, and not to referre themselves to the opinion or credit of other men; if they would avoid being deceived.

Of all prejudices, there is not any to be observed, more proper for this designe, than that which men commonly conceive of the inequality of the two Sexes.

Indeed, if we consider them in their present condition, we may observe them more different in their civil functions, and those which depend on the mind, than in such as belong to the body. And if we search for the reason of this in ordinary discourse, we find, that in[2] all the World, those that have Learning, and those that have none, and even *Women* themselves agree, to say, that they have no share in Sciences nor Employments, because that they are not capable thereof; that they have not the parts of men, and that they ought in all things be inferiour to them as they are.

After having tryed this opinion, according to the Rule of Verity, which is to admit of nothing for truth, but what is supported by clear, and distinct Notions; On the one hand it hath appeared false, and grounded on a prejudice, and Popular tradition; and on the other we have found that both Sexes are equal; that is to say, that *Women* are as noble, as perfect, and as capable as men. This cannot be established, but by refuting two sorts of adversaries; the vulgar, and almost all the learned.

The former having no other ground for what they believe, but Custome; and some slight appearances: the best way to confute them, seems to be, to let them see how that *Women* have been Subjected, and excluded from Sciences, and Employments; and having led them through the Principal conditions, and occurences of life, give them occasion to acknowledge, that *Women* have advantages which render[3] them equal to men; and this is the designe of the first part of this Treatise.

The second is employed to shew, that all the arguments of the learned are vain. And having established the Sentiment of equality, by positive reasons, *Women* are Justified from the defects of which they are ordinarily accused, by making appear that they are either imaginary, or of little importance; that they proceed only from the education which is given them, and that they mark in them considerable advantages.

This Subject may be handled two wayes, either in a flourishing, brisk, and complementive Stile, or otherwayes after the manner of Philosophers by Principles, to the end of being instructed therein to the bottom.

Such as have the true idea of eloquence, know well that these two stiles are almost inconsistent together, and that one cannot enlighten the mind, and tickle it by the same Methode. It is not but that the flourish may be joyned with reason; but that such a mixture often hinders the end which ought to be proposed in discourse, which is to convince, and perswade, that which is pleasing, musing the mind, and not suffering it to rest on what is solid.

And as men have peculiar regards for *Women*, if in a treatise made on their Subject, we mingle any thing that is gallant and courtly, those that read it, pursue their thoughts too far, and lose sight of that which ought chiefly to affect them.

Wherefore there being nothing in the World that concerns *Women* more than this designe, where we are obliged to speak in their favour, matters of the greatest force, and verity, as far as the capriciousness of the World can suffer it; we thought that it behooved us to speak seriously, and give notice thereof, lest that the conceit, that it might be a peece of airy Gallantry, should make it slightly perused, or rejected by scrupulous persons.

We are not ignorant, that this discourse will render a great many male contented,[4] and that they whose Interests and Maximes are contrary to what is proposed here, will not fail to cry out against it. To give means to answer to their complaints, we advertise persons of Spirit, and particularly the *Women* who are not the Spaniels of those that take authority over them, that if they give themselves the trouble to read this Treatise, with the attention at least that the variety of matters therein contained does require, they will observe that the Essential Character of truth, is clearness, and evidence, Which may serve them to know whether the objections that may be adduced against them be considerable or not.

And they may remark, that the most specious shall be made to them by people whose profession seems at this day to engage them to renounce experience, common sense, and themselves, that they may blindly embrace all that agrees with their prejudices, and interests, and oppugne all kinds of Truths that seem to oppose them.

And we pray consider, that the bad effects, which a panick fear may make them apprehend from this enterprise, may never perhaps happen in one single *Woman*, and that they are counterpoised with a great advantage, which may redound there-from; there being perhaps no way more natural, or sure, to draw the greatest part of *Women* from idleness, to which they are reduced, and the inconveniences that attend it, than to perswade them to study, which is almost the sole thing in which Ladies at present can imploy themselves, by making them know that they are as proper thereto as men.

And as there are none but unreasonable men, who abuse the advantages that custome hath given them, to the prejudice of *Women*; neither can there be likewise any, but indiscreet *Women*, that should make use of this peece, to make them rise against men, who would treat them as their companions, and equals. In fine, if any one be Choaked with this discourse, for what reason soever it be, let him quarrel with Truth, and not the Author: and to free himself from peevishness, let him say to himself, that it is but an Essay of wit: it is certain, that this jurk of imagination or a like, hindering truth from gaining upon us, renders it much less uneasie to those who have pain to suffer it.

The Translator
To The Unprejudiced Reader

I WELL fore-see, that my pains, in making this ingenious *French Author* speak *English*, will, according
to the bias of prejudiced, and interested humours,
undergoe various Censures; a great many men, especially
those who defie the *French*, with their Shop-tooles, will be at
it Tooth and Nail, and cry out, that so many out-landish
Trinckioms[5] having already crept into use amongst the
Women; he that would endeavour to introduce more, is no
friend to the liberty of the Subject. But such men do but hunt
their own shadow; my intent by this Translation being quite
contrary.

When I Considered, that of all Nations, The *English* did
most candidly assert, and sutably entertain the worth of the
lovely Sex; and by civility, and good nature, as well as prudence, and justice, freely grant an equality to *Women*, in all
things wherein established, and unalterable customes might
not be violated; which strangers, even the *French* themselves,
the great complimenters of that Sex, do by the force of *Philosophy*, and with reasons which wrestle against prejudices, but
at most discourse of. I thought I could not do less for the Satisfaction of such *English Men*, who do not understand my

Author in his own Language, than to make him intelligible, and so give them opportunity to infer from his opinions; that what in this matter the *Virtuosi*, and enquirers of that Nation, Squeeze from subtile Speculation, and Logick, is no more than what every *English Man* Practiseth by common sense, and Natural inclination. And herein I hope not at all to have offended that Sex.

I think I have no great reason to apprehend ill will from the *Vertuous Women*, for my endeavours of letting them hear strangers speak in their favours; since they may Lawfully conclude from thence, that if they enjoy more than their Neighbours of what is their acknowledged due, it must be their peculiar advantages beyond others, that makes them more considerable in the eyes of their Judges: there being no Countrey which produceth *Women*, who ought more Justly to boast of the favours, and endowments of nature, in respect of body and mind, than this; or who more fully enjoy, or modestly use the priviledges which upon that account, are reasonably allowed them.

This I conceive may be sufficient to warrant my undertaking, especially seeing so candid a peece of *Philosophy*, may in a great measure vindicate the honour of the Nation, (which much grieves to be imposed upon by the modes, and punctilio's of the *French* so much in fashion) by letting the world see, that the *English*, Nobly complying with that Justice which is therein so strongly pleaded for; do in matters of importance give an Example so truly Imitable, that the more ingenious must impute it to Salick Lawes, long Custome, masculine, and harsh constitutions, that they are not Universally proposed as patterns.

It is not my province to attempt the answering of objections, which may be made against this kind of *Doctrine*; both since my *Author*, whose task it was, hath fully done it; and that there is no great danger of inconveniencies, here to publish that which is already believed and put in practice. And therefore, if any corrupt minded sales-man, who may pretend to know *Women* better than either the *Author* or my self, because he hath seen more in their Bodices, shall unlace and let

flie a document,[6] and tell me that in this medling generation I
have been a little too pragmatical to follow the steps of a
stranger, and tread upon snailes when they show their hornes;
I am so innocent as not to reply, but leave him in his chase,
to be convinced by reason, and a good wife: and speak a word
to the impartial reader by way of advertisement concerning
the Treatise.

The *Author* himself gives his Reason, why he hath handled this Subject in so serious a manner, and in so short, and
Doctrinal a stile: So that I need say no more, but as a faithful
Translator, I have stuck to his words, and sense. I resolved
indeed to have accomodated this Treatise as much as possibly I could to the manners, and present customes of this nation; but finding therein, somethings whereon the *Author*
does insist as material to the establishing of his opinion,
which are not well known in this Kingdome, there being no
order of People, nor publick houses here, which in every
thing runs Parallel with NUNS, ABBESSE, and MONASTERIES,[7] but
especially with those whom he mentions: I thought it convenient to translate his words Literally, and for the understanding of one passage, which may seem difficult, advertise the
Reader, that there is an order of *Nuns* at Paris, who, because
they make it their business to relieve, and supply prisoners,
and other indigent persons, have the name of *Charity*; and
that in the great Hospital the *L'Hotel dieu* there, which is indeed a great Theatre of Humane infirmities; all the sick are
attended by Religious *Women*. If the Reader be herewith satisfied I have done my designe; and if not, I shall not, I hope,
lose the name of a friend, which is,

A. L.

The First Part

*Wherein is shewn, That the Vulgar Opinion is Prejudicated;
and that, comparing (impartially) that which may be remarked in
the Conduct of Men, and Women, we are obliged to acknowledge
an intire Equality between both Sexes.*

*M*EN perswade themselves of very many things, for which they can give no Reason; because their Assurance is founded onely upon slight Appearances, by which they suffer themselves to be hurried: and would have as strongly believed the contrary, if the Impressions of Sense or Custom had thereto determined them after the same manner.

Setting aside a small number of Learned, all the world hold, as a thing unquestionable, That the Sun moves about the Earth: Though that which appears in the Revolution of Dayes, and Years, equally inclineth those (who attentively consider) to think, That it is the Earth that takes its course round the Sun. Men imagine, that in Beasts, there is a certain Knowledge that guides them, by the same reason that wild Savages fancy, some little Spirits to be within Clocks, and other Engines which are shown them; where of they understand not the Fabrick, or Movements.

Had we been brought up in the midst of the Seas, without having ever come Ashore, we should not have failed, to have believed (as Children do when they put off in Boats), that in our Floating-houses, the Land went from us. Every one esteems his own Countrey the best, because there he is most accustomed; and that the Religion, wherein he hath been Nursed, is the True, which he ought to follow; although he hath never perhaps dream'd of examining, or comparing the same with others. We find our selves alwayes more in-clined for our Countrey-men, than for Strangers, even in mat-ters where Right is on their side. We are more pleased to Converse with those of our own Profession, than others; though neither their Wit, nor Vertue, be so great. And the Disparity of Estates and Conditions, make many judge, that Men amongst themselves are altogether unequal.

If we enquire into the ground of all these diverse Opin-ions, we shall find them bottom'd on Interest, or Custom; and that it is incomparably more difficult, to draw Men from such Sentiments, wherein they are engaged by Prejudice, than from the Opinions which they have embraced upon the Mo-tive of the strongest, and most convincing Arguments.

Amongst these odd Opinions, we may reckon the com-mon Judgement which Men make of the Difference of the two Sexes, and of all that depends thereon; there is not any mistake more Antient, or Universal. For, both the Knowing and Ignorant, are so prepossessed with the Opinion,[8] That Women are inferiour to Men in Capacity and Worth, and that they ought to be placed in that dependance wherein we see them; that the contrary Sentence will not miss to be eyed, as a Paradox, and piece of Singularity.[9]

However, for the Establishing of it, it would not at all be necessary, to use any positive Reason; if Men were more just, and less interested in their Judgements, it might suffice to advertise them, That hitherto the difference of the Sexes (to the disadvantage of the Female), hath been but very lightly discoursed of;[10] and that to judge soundly, whether our Sex have obtained any Natural Pre-eminence beyond theirs: we ought to think thereon seriously, and without Partiality, re-jecting all which hath been hitherto believed upon the simple Report of other Men, without Tryal, or Examination.

It is certain, that if a Man would set himself in this State of Indifferency, and Neutrality, he must acknowledge (on the one hand) that it is Weakness and Precipitancy that make us reckon Women less Noble and Excellent, than our selves: and that certain Natural Indispositions render them obnoxious to the Failings, and Imperfections that are attributed to them; and thereby contemptible to many. And, on the other hand, he must see, That these very Colours which cheat People concerning their own Subjects, when they slightly pass them over, would serve to undeceive them, if they sounded them a little deeper. In short, if that Man were a philosopher, he would find that there are Natural Reasons, which invincibly prove, that both Sexes are a like, both as to Body, and Soul.

But as there are not many Persons, in a condition of themselves, to put in Practice this Advice; so it must remain useless, without some pains be taken to labour with Men, and to put them in the way of making use of it. And seeing the Opinion of those who have less studied is the most general, with it we shall begin our Enquiry.

Let every Man (in particular) be asked his Thoughts of Women (in general) and that he would surely confess his Mind; he will tell you without doubt, That they were not made but for Man; That they are fit for nothing, but to Nurse; and Breed little Children in their Low Age; and to mind the House. It may be the more Ingenious will add, That there are many Women that have indeed Parts, and Conduct; but that even they who seem to have most, when they are nearly examined, discover still some-what that speaks their Sex: That they have neither Solidity, nor Constancy; nor that depth of Judgement which they think to find in themselves: And that it hath been an Effect of Divine Providence, and Wisdom of Men, to have barred them from Sciences, Government, and Offices: That it would be a pleasant thing indeed, to see a Lady in the Chair (in quality of a Professor) teaching *Rhetorick*, or *Medicine*; marching along the Streets, followed by Officers, and Sergeants; putting in Execution Lawes: Playing the part of a Counsellour; pleading before Judges: Seated on a Bench, to Administer Justice in Supream

Courts: Leading of an Army; giving Battel; and Speaking before States, and Princes, as the Head of an Embassy.

I do confess, such Practices would surprize us; but for no other reason, but that of Novelty. For, if in modelling of States, and establishing the different Offices that compose them, Women had been like-wise called to Functions; we should have been as much accustomed to have seen them in Dignity, as they are to see us. And should have found it no more strange to have seen a Lady on a Throne, than a Woman in a Shop.

If these Blades[11] be pressed a little further, we shall find their mightiest Arguments reduced to this, That, as to Women, matters have alwayes past as now they go; which is a mark, that they are really such, as they are esteemed: And that, if they had been capable of Sciences,[12] and Offices, Men would not have denied them their shares.

These kind of Reasonings proceed from the Conceit that we have of the Equity of our Sex; and a false Notion which Men forge to themselves of Custom: It is enough with them to find that a thing is established, to make them believe it well grounded. And as they judge, that men ought to do nothing without Reason; so the most part of People cannot imagine, but that Reason hath been consulted for the introducing of such Practises, as they see universally received; and fancy to themselves, that Prudence, and right Reason, have established the Customes, to which they both oblige us to conforme; since, without breach of Order, we cannot therein dispence with our Obedience.

Every one sees (in his own Countrey) the Women in such Subjection, that, in all things, they depend on Men, without being admitted to Learning; or any of those Conditions, that afford opportunity to become remarkable by the advantage of[13] Parts: No Body affirms, that he hath ever seen them treated other-wise. And all know, That matters go so with them every where, that there is no place in the World, where they are not used after the same manner, as we find at Home. In some Countries their Usage is worse, where they are regarded as Slaves. In *China* they keep their Feet little from their Child-hood, to hinder them from rambling out of Doors; where they never see any thing but their Husbands, and Children. In *Turkey* the Ladies are strictly enough confined; And in *Italy* they are not much better. Almost all the People of *Asia, Affrica,* and *America,* use their Wives, as we do our Serving-Maids. They are no where imployed in any thing, but that which is esteemed low, and base: And because they only discharge the lesser care of Hus-wivery and Nurses, Men commonly perswade themselves, that, for that end alone they are in the World; and that they are uncapable of any thing else: They cannot easily represent to themselves how matters would be other-wayes; it appearing impossible to alter them, what endeavour soever be used.

The wisest Law-givers in founding their Common-Wealths have established nothing on this Account, in favour of Women. All their Laws seem only to have been made to confirm Men in the Possession they have got. Most part of Men, who have passed for Learned, have not said any thing to the advantage of Women: And the Conduct of Men, in all Ages, and Places of the World, appears so uniform in this case, that it seems they have conspired; or other-wayes (as many imagine) have been led thereunto by a secret Instinct; that is to say, Letters-Patent from the Author of Nature.[14]

Men are still the more perswaded in this, when they consider in what manner the Women (themselves) support this their Condition. They look upon it as a thing natural to them; whether it be that they reflect not upon what they are; or that being born, and bred in dependence, they make the same Judgement thereon, as Men do. Now, upon all these views, the one, and the other, let themselves believe, both, That their Spirits are as different as their Bodies; and that there ought to be as great distinction betwixt the two Sexes, in all the Functions of Life, as there is in those which are peculiar to either: Whilst,[15] in the mean-time, that perswasion (like the most part of those which we draw from Use, and Custom,) is nothing but Prejudice, formed in us by the appearances of things, for want of closer Examination; and of which we might easily undeceive our selves, if we would but take the pains to return back to the Fountain-head, and judge in many Occurencies of that which hath been done in former times, by what is practised at this day; and of the Custom of the Antients, by what we see in Vogue in our own times: Had Men followed this Rule in many of their Sentiments, they had not so easily fallen into mistakes. And as to what concerns the present state of Women, they would have acknowledged, that they have not been subjected by any other Law, than that of the stronger; and that it hath not been for want of Natural Capacity, or Merit, that they have not shared with us in that which raises our Sex above theirs.

Indeed, when we consider seriously the Affairs of this World, both past, and present, we find that all agree in this, That Reason hath always been the weakest: And it seems, that Histories have only been composed, to Demonstrate that which every one sees in his own time, That ever since there hath been Men in the World, force hath always prevailed. The greatest Empires of *Asia*, in their beginnings, have been the work of Usurpers, and Thieves. And the scattered Wracks of the *Grecian*, and *Roman* Monarchies, have not been gathered, but by those who thought themselves strong enough to resist their Masters, and domineer over their Equals. This Conduct is no less visible in all other Societies. And if Men behave themselves so towards their Fellows, there is great likely-hood from Stronger Reason, That, in the beginning, they have done so, every one towards his Wife. And this is almost the manner how it hath happened.

Men observing, that they were the stronger, and that in relation of Sex, they have some advantage of Body, fancyed that they had the same in all; the Consequence was not great for Women in the beginning of the World, Affairs being in a Condition far different from what now they are: when neither Government, Science, Office, nor Religion, were established, the Notion of Dependence had in it nothing at all of Irksome. I Imagine that Men lived then like little Children, and all the Advantage that was, was like that of Play. Men and Women (who then were simple, and innocent) were equally employed in labouring of the Land, or Hunting, (as the Wild *Indians* do at this day): The Man took his Course and the Woman her's; And they that brought Home most Profit, were commonly most esteemed.

The Inconveniencies that attend and follow the big-Belly,[16] weakening the strength of the Female for some Interval[17] of time, and hindering them to labour as formerly, required (necessarily) the Assistance of their Husbands; and the more still, whil'st they were taken up with the care of their young Children. This produced some Regards of Esteem, and Preferrence in Families, which then were only composed of Father, Mother, and some little Babes: But when Families began to be enlarged; and that in the same House, lived not only the Father, but the Father's Mother, the Children's Children; with Brothers, and Sisters, Elder and younger: Then did Dependence dilate it self, and become more sensible: Then was to be seen, the Mistriss submitting to her Husband, the Son honouring his Father, and he commanding his Children. And as it is most difficult for Brothers, alwayes, perfectly to agree; we may easily conceive, that they lived not long together, before that some Difference hapned amongst them: The Elder, stronger than the rest, would condescend to them in nothing: So, Force obliged the Lesser to bow under the Greater, and the Daughters to follow the Example of their Mother.

It is easie to be imagined, that in such Families, there were then several different Functions; That the Women, being bound to stay at Home to bring up their Children, took the Care within Doors: The Men (more free and strong) charged themselves with the Affairs abroad; and that after the Death of the Father and Mother, the First-Born took upon him the Government. The Daughters, accustomed to the House, had no thoughts of going abroad; but some Younger Brothers, discontented, and more fierce than they, refusing to submit to the Yoak, were obliged to withdraw, and set up for themselves: And so, several of the same Humour meeting together, made a shift to live on their Fortunes, and easily contracted Friendship: Who, finding themselves without Estate, sought out means to purchase what they wanted: and seeing there was no other way but to take from their Neighbours, they fell upon that which came next to hand: And, to confirm themselves in the Possession of their New Conquests, at the same time made themselves Masters of the owners.

The voluntary Dependence, which was before in Families, ceased by this Invasion; Fathers and Mothers, with their Children, being constrained to obey an unjust Usurper: So that, the Condition of Women became harder than before. For, as till then, they had never been married but to Men of their own House, and Family; they were afterward forced to take Strangers, and unknown Husbands, who only considered them as the loveliest part of their Booty.

It is ordinary with Conquerours, to despise those amongst the Subdued, whom they judge the weakest: And the Women appearing to be such, by reason of their Employments (which required not much Strength), were looked upon as inferiour to Men.

Some there were who contented themselves with this first Usurpation; but others, more ambitious, (encouraged by the success of their Victory) resolved to proceed in their Conquests. The Women being more humane, than to serve such unjust Designes, were left at Home; and the Men chosen as the most proper for such Enterprizes, where there is need of Force. In this state of Life matters being no other-wayes esteemed, but as Men thought them useful to the ends which they proposed; and the desire of Dominion being now become the strongest of Passions, which could not be satisfied but by Violence, and Injustice; of which, men were the only Instruments: It is no wonder that they were preferred to Women. Men like-wise, serving to maintain the Conquests which they had made: Their Counsels were only taken for to establish their Tyranny, because none were so[18] fit to put them in Execution. And so, the Mildness, and Humanity of Women, was the sole cause which excluded them from having any share in the Administration of Publick Government.

The Example of Princes was quickly imitated by their Subjects, every one would carry it over his Companion; and private men[19] began to rule more absolutely in their Families.

So soon as a Lord found himself Master of a People, and considerable Countrey, he shaped it into a Kingdom, made Laws
for Government, chose his Officers from amongst the Men;
and raised to Places those who had best served him in his
Enterprizes. So notable a Preference[20] of one Sex above the
other, lessened still more the Esteem for the Women; and
their Humour and Course of Life, being far from Butchery,
and Warr; Men believed them no other-wayes capable to contribute to the Safety and Preservation of Kingdomes, but
only by helping to people them.

States and Common-Wealths could not be established,
without the placing of some Distinction amongst those that
did compose them: So Marks of Honour were introduced for
distinguishing of Orders, and Signes of Respect invented to
testifie the Difference, which was acknowledged to be
amongst Men. And to the Notion of Power, was added the
External Submission, which is commonly rendred to those
who have the Authority in their Hands.

It is not at all necessary to tell you, how *God* hath been
known of Men; but it is certain, that since the beginning of
the World, he hath been adored by them; though the Worship
which Men have rendred to a *Deity*, was never Regular, but
since they were assembled in Bodies to make up Publick
Societies.

Now, as Men were accustomed to Reverence the Powers, by External Marks of Respect; they thought it like-wise
their Duty, to Reverence *God* by some Ceremonies, which
might serve to manifest the Sentiments which they entertained of his Greatness. Temples were built, Sacrifices appointed, and Men (who were already the Heads of Government) failed not also, to take to themselves, the care of that
which concerned Religion. And Custom having now prepossessed the Women with an Opinion that all belonged to Men,
they contented[21] themselves without aspiring to any part of
the Publick Ministry. But the *Idea* which Men conceived of a
God-Head, being extreamly corrupted by the Fables and Fic-
tions of Poets, they forged to themselves Divinities, both
Male and Female; and appointed, Shee-*Priests* for the Service

of those of their Sex; but still with Subordination to the Conduct, and Pleasure of their *Priests*.

Women have been likewise known to have Governed great States; but we must not imagine, that it was because they have been called thereto out of a purpose of Restitution of their right; but because they had the Dexterity so to dispose of Affairs, that *Men* could not snatch the Authority out of their Hands.

It is true, there are at this day Hereditary States, where the *Females* succeed to *Males*, as Queens, or Princesses; But we have no reason to believe, but that if *Men* have suffered the Scepter to fall into the place of the Distaffe, it was only that they might prevent the People from falling together by the Ears;[22] And that, if they have permitted *Female* Regencies, it was in consideration, that the Mothers (who always extreamly love their Children) would take a more particular Care of their States during their Minority.

So that, now the *Women* being other-wayes imployed, but in their Huswivery, and finding therein business enough; let us not think it strange, that they have not invented any of those Sciences; whereof the greatest part (at first) have been but the work, and task of some idle Loyterers.

The *Aegyptian Priests* (who had not much to do) busied themselves in chatting together, concerning the Effects of Nature, which seemed most to touch them: And after much talking and reasoning, began to make Observations; the noise of which, stirred up the Curiosity of some *Men* to come in search of them: But Sciences being but then in the Cradle, did not allure the *Women* out of Doors. Besides, that the Jealousie which already imbroyled the Husbands would have filled them with Suspition, that their Wives had gone to visit the *Priests* rather for Love to their Persons, than Learning which they had obtained.

After that several *Men* had received some tincture of this new Learning, they began to assemble themselves in certain Places, to discourse thereof more at leisure; where every one speaking his Thoughts, Knowledge ripened, and Colledges and Accademies were appointed, where the *Women* were not admitted; but in the same manner were excluded from Learning, as they had been from all the rest.

Notwithstanding, the Restraint wherein they were kept, hindred not, but that some of them procured the Conversation and Writings of the Learned; whereby (in a short time) they equalled the progress of the most Ingenious: But Custome having already enjoyed an impertinent *Decorum*, that *Men* durst not come to their Houses, nor other *Women* visit them for fear of giving some umbrage, they made no Disciples, nor founded Sects; but all the Light which they had attained, uselessly, dyed with themselves.

If we observe how Modes and Fashions creep into use, and how they are dayly imbelished, we may judge, That (in the beginning of the World) People took no great care of their Dress: All was then simple and plain, nothing minded but necessity. *Men* flea'd Beasts; and fastening their Skins together, framed to themselves Habits. But afterwards, Commodiousness began to be devised; and every one accowtering themselves according to their fancy, the Fashions that were most decent, were presently followed; and they that were under the same Prince, strove to conform themselves to his Mode.

It happened not so with Modes and Fashions, as with Governments and Sciences; the *Women* here had their share with *Men*: who perceiving them by their dress more lovely, took no care to rob them thereof. And both the one, and the other, finding that some sort of Apparel set off more gracefully, and rendred more amiable the Person, both strove to find out the Knack: But the Employments of *Men* being greater, and more important, hindered them from the more eager Pursuit.

The *Women* herein shewed their Prudence, and Skill; For, observing that new Ornaments made them more agreeable, and dear to *Men*, and thereby their Condition more supportable; they neglected nothing which they thought might serve to render themselves Charming, and Lovely. To that end, they employed Gold, Silver, and Precious Stones, as soon as they grew in Vogue: And seeing that *Men* had deprived them of Means, to make themselves Conspicuous by their Parts, they applyed themselves solely to find out that which might render them amiable, and pleasing. In this they have very well succeeded: For, their Beauty, and Attire, have advanced them to greater Esteem in the Eyes of *Men*, than all the Books and Learning of the World could ever have done. This Custom hath been too well Established, to admit of any future Change; the Practice thereof, hath continued to our times; and it seems to be a Tradition too antient to be now contradicted, or opposed.

In appears clearly (from this Historical Conjecture), That, according to the manner of dealing familiar to all *Men*, it is only by Force and Empire that they have reserved to themselves these Extrinsical[23] Advantages; from which, the Female Sex is debarred. For, to warrant them to say, That it hath been grounded on Reason, they must never have communicated them amongst themselves, but to those who have been most capable; Always made the Choice of such with exact Scrutiny, and Discretion: Never have admitted to study, but such as they knew disposed for Letters: Never raised to Charges, but those that were fittest for Employment; and excluded all others. And, in short, Never have set any *Man*, on any thing, but what was suitable to his Inclinations.

We see the contrary daily put in Practice; For, there is nothing but Chance, Necessity, or Interest, which engageth *Men* in the different Conditions and States of Civil Society. The Children learn their Father's trade, because that it hath alwayes been mentioned to them. One is forced to the Gown, who would have been better pleased with the Sword, had it been at his own choice: and the ablest *Man* in the World shall never enter into Employment, if he want Money to buy his Place. How many are there groveling in the dust, who would have made themselves famous, had they been but in the way? and how many Clowns are there, that might have become great Doctors had they been sent to School? We have but little ground to pretend that the present *Virtuosi* are only such of the times, who have the best Genius for the things wherein they excell; and that, amongst so many Persons buried in

Ignorance, there are none who, with the same means which they have had, could have rendered themselves more capable.

Why is it then, that we assure ourselves, that Women are less fit for such things than our selves? sure it is not Chance, but Unavoidable necessity that hinders them from playing their parts. I urge not, that all Women are capable of all Sciences and Employments; that any one is capable of all: No *Man* pretends to so much; but I only desire, that, considering the Sex in general, we may acknowledge an aptitude in the one as well as the other.

Let us but glance a little upon that, which we see dayly in the play and smaller divertisements of Children. The Girles show therein a more gentile air, more of Wit, and greater dexterity: And when fear or shame does not stifle their Humours, their Discourse, is more ingenious, and pleasant; and their conversation more lively, brisk, and free: They Learn sooner what they are taught, if they be equally played: They are more industrious, more painfull, more submiss, more modest, and more reserved; In a word, we may remarke in them,[24] in a more eminent degree, all those excellent qualities, which being found in young Men, make them esteemed fitter for high matters, than those who are otherwise their equalls.

Notwithstanding that, that which appeares, in the two Sexes, whilst they are as yet in the cradle, is sufficient to make us conclude, that the more lovely gives also the fairest hopes; yet men take no notice thereof; Masters and Teaching are onely for the Men: Particular care is taken to instruct them in all which is thought proper, to form and improve the mind;[25] whilst in the mean time, the Women are let languish in Idleness, Softness, and Ignorance: Or, otherwise grovel in low, and base imployments.

But for all this, we need but two eyes to perceive, that the case of the two Sexes is just like that of two Brothers, in the same family; Where the younger, notwithstanding of the neglect of his breeding, makes often appear, that the elder has no advantage over him, but the start in coming into the World.

For what end serves commonly the Education which is given to Men? It is useless to a great many for the proposed end: Nor does it hinder, but that many fall into vice, and dissolution: And that others remain still ignorant, and even many times become greater Fops than they were before. If they had before any thing of breeding,[26] of briskness or civility, they lose it by their study. All goes against them, and they against all things; So that one would say, that they had spent their youth in traveling in Forraign Countreys where they had only frequented the Society of Salvages; so much Clownishness, and rudeness of manners they bring home with them. All that they have Learned is like goods of Contreband, which they either cannot or dare not vend: And if they have a mind to venture into the World again, and therein appear as they ought, they are obliged to go to School to the Ladyes, there to learn garb and complaisance; and all that out-side which now adayes compleats a Gentleman.

If we come nearer, and consider this: Instead of undervaluing the Women, because they have no great Stock of Learning, we should the rather esteem them happy: Since that if on the one hand they are thereby destitute of the means to set off the parts, and advantages which are peculiar to them[27] on the other hand, they have not the occasion to spoile or lose them: Who, notwithstanding that defect, advance in Vertue, Wit, and good Grace as fast as they grow in Years. So that, should we without prejudice, or a byassed Judgement, compare young men when they come new off of the press,[28] with the Women of their own age; and not know how either the one or the other had been bred, we could not but believe, their education to have been quite contrary.

The out-side alone, the air of the face, the looks, the gate, the countenance, and the gestures, in Women, speak somewhat 'posed,[29] grave, and discreet, which sufficiently distinguisheth them from men; none can be more reserved than they, words of double meaning never escape their lips, the smallest equivocation wounds their ears, nor can they endure the sight of any thing that choaks modesty.

The Conduct of most men is of a quite different stamp.
Their March is often rash, and precipitant; their gestures odd
and Antick, their eyes Rambling and un-settled: and are
never more pleased than when they are entertained and fed
with things which ought either be kept silent or hid.

Let us but converse a little with Women, and that which
the world call the Learned, either in company together, or a
part by themselves, and we shall see the difference that is between the one and other. One would say that the men had
stuffed their heads with study, that they might Clogg, and
confound their Wits. Nothing comes clearly from them, and
the pain that they put themselves to, to pump for the words,[30]
quite spoils the rellish of that which they might have said to
purpose; So that unless the natural Wit be good, or they in
company with men of their one Gang, hardly can they entertain an houres-Discourse.

Women on the contrary, express neatly, and in order,
what they conceive: Their words cost them nothing; they begin, and go on at their pleasure, and when they have their liberty, their fancy supplies them alwayes with inexhaustible lib-
erality. They have the gift of proposing their thoughts, with a
sweetness, and complacency that insinuates as strongly as
Reason: When men on the other hand, do it in a manner
rough and dry.

Let any Questions be started in presence of Women of
clearer Wit, they have presently the point that is drove at;
They consider it under more appearances: What is said to
purpose, finds sooner acceptance in their minds; And when
that we are a little known to them, and that they have no suspition of us, we find their prejudices not so strong as those of
men; nor they thereby so armed against the truth proposed.
They are altogether averse from contradiction, and dispute,
to which the learned are so addicted: they nibble not vainly at
words, nor make use of the Scientifick, and Mysterious terms
which are so proper to cover Ignorance; but all what they say
is sense and intelligible.

I have taken delight to entertain my self with Women, of
all the different conditions that I could meet-with, both in the

Town, and Countrey; to the end, that I might discover the best, and the worst; and I have found amongst those of them whom necessity, and labour, had not rendred stupid, more sound judgement than in the most part of the workes, which pass with great credit among the vulgarly learned of the age.[31]

In speaking concerning God, it never entered into one of their heads to tell me, that she conceived Him, under the shape of a venerable old man: On the contrary, they said, that they would not imagine, (that is) represent him to themselves, under any appearance like to men: That they conceived there was a God, because they could not comprehend that they themselves, or that all other things which did environ them, could be the work of chance, or of any creature: and that the conduct of their affairs being no effect of their prudence, because that the success thereof rarely answered the wayes, and methods, which they had taken; it must needs be the effect of Divine Providence.

When I asked them, What they thought of their Souls; they never made me answer: *That it is* a very subtile, and thin flame, or a disposition of the Organs of their Bodyes; nor that it was capable of extension, or contraction. On the contrary, they answered, that they perceived very well, that it was distinct from their bodyes; And that the greatest certainty that they could say thereof, was that they believed it altogether unlike any of those things, which they perceived by Sense; but that if they had been Book-learned, they should have known to a Hair[32] what it was.

It never entereth into the Head of a Nurse, to say as Physitians do, that their Sick began to be better, because the Concoctive Faculty performs (laudably) its Functions: And when they see a great Quantity of Blood stream from a Vein, they laugh at those who deny a Communication of the others there-with by Circulation.

When I would know of them, Why it was that they believed, that the Stones exposed to the *Sun*, and *Southern*-Showers, did sooner weare, than those that lay to the *North*? There was not simple enough to Answer me, That it comes to pass by reason that the *Moon* gnawes them with sharp Teeth, as some *Philosophers* pleasantly fancy; but that (they being dryed up by the Heat of the *Sun*) the following Showers made them the more easily moulder.

I have demanded (at least) of twenty for the nonce, If they believed not that *God* (by an Obediential, or Extraordinary Power) could elevate a Stone to the Beatifick Vision? But could never draw from them any other Answer, but that they thought, I jested with them by such a kind of Question.

The greatest Fruit that we can expect from Learning, is a just Discerning, and exactitude in Distinguishing of that which is true and evident, from what is false and obscure; thereby to avoid falling into Errour, or Mistake. People are easily inclined to believe, that Men (at least such as pass for Knowing) have in this the better of the Women. Nevertheless, if we have but a little of that Discerning and Exactitude of which I spake, we shall find that it is one of the Qualities they want most; For, they are not only obscure, and confused in their Discourses, (by which good Quality they often sway, and attract the Belief of simple and credulous Persons); but they even reject that which is evident, and scoff at those who speak in a manner clear and intelligible, as too easie and common: They fall first upon any Obscurity proposed to them, as being the most Mysterious of the rest. To Convince them of this, we need do no more but hear them with a little Patience; and afterward, oblige them to explain themselves.

The Women are of an Humour very far from this. We may observe, that such as have a little seen the World, cannot endure that even their own Children should speak *Latin* in their Presence; they mistrust others that do so; and often say, That they are afraid lest some Impertinency be hid under such strange Attires.

We never hear them meddle with the Sacred Terms of Arts, as Men call them; Nay, they cannot be made so much as get them by Heart, though their Memories be very good, and that they have heard them often repeated. And when we speak to them in obscure and hard Words, they frankly confess, that they want Wit and Understanding to reach our Meaning; or other wise, they well perceive, that such as Cant after that manner, want Knowledge and Learning to speak other-wise.

In fine, if we consider the several wayes and methods, whereby the Men, and the Women, bring forth what they know; we must judge, that the one are like to Labourers that work in Quarries, who (with great Pain) win from thence rude and shapeless Stones; And that the Women (like skillful Architects, and Masons)[33] polish, and fitly place in Work, what they have put into their Hands.

We find an infinite number of *Women*, who not only Judge of things with as much Exactness, as if they had had the most exquisite Education; without either Prejudices, or confused Notions (the ordinary stumbling-Block of the Learned); but also, see many, that (with a Judgement cleer and just) can Discourse of the Objects of the most Refined Sciences, as if they had alwayes studied them.

They express their Minds with a Grace; and have the Knack by hitting on the best Terms in use, to speak more with one word than *Men* can do with many. If we Discourse with them of Languages in general, they have that pitch of Thoughts which is not to be found but in the ablest *Grammarians*: And, in short, They are observed to draw more from Custom alone, for the embellishing of their Language, than the most part of *Men* from Study and Practice both together.

Eloquence is a Talent so natural, and peculiar to them, that no Body can dispute it: They perswade what they please; and can Indite and Defend without the help of Laws: So that, there are but few Judges, who have not proved them the most prevalent Proctors. Can there be anything more weighty, or Elegant, than the Letters of several Ladies upon all the Subjects that fall under ordinary Conversation, and principally upon the Passions? The Movements of which, make up all the beauty and secret of *Rhetorick*. They handle them with so delicate a Touch, and express them so Naturally, that we are obliged to confess, that we feel them to be such as they speak them; and that all the Oratory of the World is not able to give to *Men*, that which costs nothing to *Women*. The Flights of

Eloquence, Poesie, Harangues, Sermons, and Discourses, soar not at all above their reach; And nothing is wanting to their Criticks, but the Rules, and a few Terms of Art.

I am not ignorant, that this Treatise it self, will not escape their Censure; and that there are many who will find fault with it: Some will condemn it, as not at all proportionate to the Grandeur, and Dignity of the Subject: That the Strain of it is not so Gallant, the Stile so Noble, nor the Expressions so Lofty and Elevated as was fit: That there are several Passages slightly handled, where many Important Remarks might have been imployed: But I hope my Good-will, and the Designe which I proposed, to speak nothing but Truth, and to avoid the forced Expressions which favour of *Romance*, will plead Excuse for me at their Hands.

They have (moreover) this Advantage, That the Eloquence of Action is in them much more lively than in *Men*: There, *Men* alone let[34] us see, that they intend to speak, as to gain the Point.

Their Air is noble and great, their Port free and Majestuous, their Carriage decent, their Gestures naturall, their Stile engaging, their Words easie, and their Voice sweet and melting. The Beauty and Grace of their Discourse (when it enters once the Mind), opens to them the Door of the Heart. If they reason of Good and Evil, on their Countenance appears that Character of Integrity, which renders the Perswasion more prevalent: And when they would excite Love for Vertue, their Heart is seen on their Lips; and the Image which they give thereof (decked with the Ornaments of Discourse and Graces, which are so peculiar to them) appears a hundred times more Lovely.

It is pretty to hear a *Woman*, that sets herself to plead; how clearly she explains, and unties all the Knots and Labyrinths of Affairs; precisely states her own, and Parties Pretensions: Discovers what hath given ground to the Suit, and the manner how she has managed it; what Engines she hath set a work in all her Proceedings; and how (in all things) she shewes a certain Capacity in Business, which is wanting to the most part of *Men*.

It is this which makes me think, that if they made it their business to study Law, they would succeed in it (at least) as well as we; But we see, that Peace and Justice is their study; With Grief they hear of Differences, and with Joy endeavour to take them up friendly: Their Care in that, makes them find out Turns, and singular Expedients, for the Reconciling of Minds; And, upon the Conduct of their own, or their Neighbours Families, they naturally make these Reflections of Equity; upon which, all the knowledge of Law and Justice is founded.

In the Rehearsals of those who are Witty, there is alwayes some pleasingness with order, which is not to be found in ours: They discern what is proper, or impertinent to the Subject; decide the interests; describe the persons, with their true and natural Characters; unfold the intrigues, and trace the greatest as well as the least, when they set thereon. This is evidently to be seen in the Histories, and Romances of ingenious Ladyes who are still alive.

How many are there that learn as much at Sermons, in Discourse, and some little books of Piety, as many Doctors with *Thomas Aquinas* in their studyes, or upon their deskes? and speak with that solidity, and depth about the highest Mysteries of all the Christian Morality; that they might often pass for great Divines, if they did but wear a hat, or could Lugg into play Latin sentences.

Women seem born to practice Physick, and to restore the sick to health; for the neatness and complying humour easeth one half of the distemper; and they are not only proper to apply remedyes, but likewise to invent: They find out an infinite number, which are commonly called Small, because they cost less than those of *Galen* or *Hippocrates*, and are not prescribed by Receit, but which are by so much the more easy, and secure, as they are simple and natural. In fine, they make their observations in their practices, with so much exactness, and they discourse thereof with so good reason; That they often render useless all the Places of the Schools.

Amongst the countrey Women, those that labour in the fields, are wonderfully skilfull in the odd, and unconstant

Freaks of Seasons; and their Almanacks are a great deal more
certain than those, which are printed from the hands of As-
trologers. They explain naturally the fertility and barrenness
of years, from the Winds, Rains, and what else is produced
by the change of Weather; so that no body can hear them discourse thereof, without pity and compassion of the Learned,
who charge all these Effects on[35] Aspects, Conjunctions, As-
cendencies of Planets and the like; which makes me think,
that if Women had been taught, that, the alterations to which
the body of man[36] is subject, might come upon him by reason
of his particular constitution, his exercise, the climate
wherein he lives, his food, education, and different occurrences of Life; they had never let it enter in their Heads, to
have referred these Various Inclinations and Changes to the
Influencies of Starrs; Bodies at so many Thousand Miles distant from us.

I confess, there are some Sciences, of which *Women* are
not at all heard to speak; because they are not the Sciences of
ordinary Vent, nor Society. *Algebra*,[37] *Geometry*, and the *Op-
ticks*, never (or rarely) leave Studies, and Learned *Academies*,
to come into the Croud. And, as their greatest use is to give
just Measures to our Thoughts, they ought not to appear in
ordinary Converse; but secretly, like hidden Springs that
move, and make great Machins Play: my Meaning is, that we
should make such Application of them in the Subjects of
Converse and Entertainment, as to think and speak truly, and
Geometrically, without making great shew of our Art.

All these Observations on the Qualities of the Mind,
may be easily gathered amongst *Women* of a middle Condition; But if we advance as far as the Court, and be admitted
into the Entertainments of Ladies, there is quite another
thing to be Remarked. It seems that their Genius is Naturally
suited to their Quality; their Quaintness, and polite Discerning, speaks a frame of Spirit, delicate, fine, and easie; and
some-what Great and Noble, which is their own. We may
say, that Objects (like *Men*) approach them with Respect;
they alwayes see them in their best Dresse, and speake of
them with an Air beyond the Common. In a word, show a

Man that has a taste, two Letters of Ladies of different Rank, and he shall easily know which of them is Highest in Quality.

How many Ladies have there been, and how many are there still, who ought to be placed amongst the number of the Learned, if we assigne them not a Higher Sphear? The Age wherein we live hath produced more of these, than all the past. And as they have in all things run parallel with *Men*, upon some Particular Reasons, they ought more to be esteemed than they: For, it behoved them to surmount the Softness wherein their Sex is bred, renounce the Pleasures and Idleness, to which Custom had condemned them, overcome certain publick Impediments that removed them from study, and to get above those disadvantagious Notions, which the Vulgar conceive of the Learned; besides, those of their own Sex in general: All this they have performed. And whether it be, that these Difficulties have rendred their Wit more quick and penetrating, or that these Qualities are peculiar to[38] their Nature, they have (proportionably) made Progress and Advancements beyond *Men*.

It may be said nevertheless (without diminishing the Sentiments which are due to such famous Ladies), that it is occasion, and External means, which hath advanced them to this State, as well as the more Learned amongst us; and that there are infinite numbers of *Women*, which could have done no less, had their Advantages been Equal.

And, seeing it is great Injustice to believe, that all *Women* are Indiscreet, because we know five or six to be so; we ought also to be so equitable, as to judge their Sex capable of Sciences, since we see many that have raised themselves to a perfection therein.

It is commonly believed amongst us, that *Turks, Barbarians*, and wild Savages, are not so proper for learning as the people of Europe; though it be certain, that if we found five or six of them here, that had the capacity or title of Doctor (which is not at all impossible) they would correct our opinion; and confess, that these being men like to our selves, they are capable of the same things; and that if they had been taught, they would not have yielded[39] to us in the least. The

Women, with whom we live, deserve surely as much as *Barbarians*, and Savages, to oblige us to entertain thoughts no less reasonable or advantagious for them.

But if the head-strong vulgar (notwithstanding these observations) will still stand upon it, that the Women are not so fit for Arts, and Sciences as we are; they ought at least to acknowledge, that they have less need of them. For it is for two ends that we apply our selves to Learning; The one, that we may attain to a true knowledge of the objects of our Sciences; and the other, that by such knowledge, we may rise to virtue: So that in this our short life, Knowledge being but the hand-Maid to Vertue;[40] and the Women in possession of this: we may conclude, that by a particular happiness, they have gained the principal advantages of Sciences, without having ever taken the pains to study them.

What we see daily, is sufficient to convince us, that they are no less Christians than men; They receive the Gospell with Simplicity and Humility; and in following the Rules and Maxims thereof, are exemplary: Their reverence towards Religion, hath alwayes appeared so great, that they are esteemed without contradiction more devout and pious than we: or, though it be true, that their worship sometimes goes too far; yet therein I cannot find them so culpable; since the ignorance wherein they have been bred, is the necessary cause of that excess. If their Zeale be undiscreet, their Perswasion is at least true; And we may affirm, that if they had a clearer sight of Vertue, they would embrace it after another manner; since they cleave to it so fast, even through obscurity and darkness itself.

It seems, that mercy and compassion which is the Vertue of the Gospel is in love with their Sex. The calamity of the Neighbour no sooner touches their mind, but it pierces their heart, and brings teares in their eyes. Is it not their hands that in publick afflictions distribute the largest Charity? And is it not at this day, the Ladys that take the particular care of the poor and sick in the parishes, visit them in prisons, and serve them in the Hospitals? Is it not these Religious Nuns, dispersed in every quarter, who have the charge at certain hours of the day, to carry to such their food, and necessary remedies; and have thereby deserved the name of that Charity, which they have so worthily practised?[41]

In fine; If there were no other Women in the world that discharged this Vertue towards their Neighbours, but those who attend the sick in that great Hospital, the *L'Hotel-Dieu* of *Paris*; I cannot think that with Justice, men could pretend to the advantage above their Sex therein. These are properly the Virgins, with whom the Galleries of the Illustrious, and Noble Women,[42] ought to be enriched: Of their life it is that we should sing the highest Elogies, and honour their death, with the most excellent Panegyricks: Since here it is that we may see the Christian Religion, that is to say, truly *Heroicke* Vertue, practised up to the rigour, both in it's precepts, and counsels; by young Virgins, who Renouncing the World and themselves, embrace a perpetual Chastity, and Poverty, take their Cross, and that the most heavy Cross of the world, and render themselves for the rest of their dayes, under the Yoak of *Jesus Christ*: Who Consecrate themselves to an Hospital, where the inffirm of all sorts, of all countreys and Religions are indifferently received, there to serve all without distinction, and to charge[43] themselves (according to the example of their Lord and Husband)[44] with all the infirmities of mankind: without being discouraged by having their eyes Continually smitten with the most horrid of Spectacles, their eares with the reproaches and cries of the sick, and their smelling with all the infectious scents of Humane putrifaction: and who, for a marke of that Spirit which does guid them, carry in their armes from bed to bed, and comfort the poor wretches, not in vain words; but by the effectual, and personal Example of patience, and invincible Charity.

Is there any thing amongst Christians to be conceived greater than this? And yet, Other *Women* are no less inclined to assist, and comfort their neighbours; they want nothing but opportunity, when other business does not divert them there-from. And I think it no less unworthy to imagine from thence, (as the vulgar commonly do) that *Women* are naturally servants to men; than to pretend that they, who have received talents, and particular endowments from God, are servants, and slaves to those, for whose good they employ them.

The conduct of *Women*, in what kind of life soever they embrace, hath alwayes somewhat remarkable. It seems that such who live single, and yet keep their freedome in the world, remain only there to be a pattern, and give example to others. Christian modesty appears in their countenance and attire, and Vertue makes their chiefest Ornament. They wholly separate themselves from worldly Conversation and pastimes; and their application to[45] the works of Piety, and Religion,[46] gives clear proof, that they have only refused the cares, and trouble of Marriage, that they might enjoy a greater liberty of mind, and be obliged to nothing else but to please God.

There are as many Monasteries under the government of *Women* as of Men, and their lives therein no less exemplary. There, the recourse is greater, the discipline no less Austere; and the Abbesses of no less worth than the Abbots. They setle Rules with so admirable Wisdome, and Govern their *Nuns* with such prudence, that seldome amongst them happens any disorder: and, in short, the fame of Religious houses, and the great Rents which they possess, are the fruits of the good order of their Superiours.

Marriage is a state of life, the most natural, and ordinary to men; when once they are ingaged therein, it is Death that must discharge them,[47] and there they spend these periods of age, where reason ought to be the chief guid, over the different accidents of Nature and Fortune (to which this Condition of Life is liable) exercising them who live therein more than others, & gives them occasion thereby to give greater tryal of their Parts.

A little Experience is sufficient to inform us, That the *Women* here are more fit and useful than we; For, young Maids are capable to order a House, at that Age when *Men* stand still in need of a Master. And the most proper Expedient to reclaim a young *Man*, and restore him to the Right Way, is, to give him a *Wife*; who may reclaim him by her Example, moderate his Extravagancies, and win him from his Debauches.

What Complyance do[48] not Wives use, that they may live peaceably with their Husbands? They submit to their Humours, do nothing without their Advice, lay constraint upon themselves in many things for fear to displease them, and even deprive themselves of honest and lawful Recreations, to free them from Suspition.

It is well enough known, which of the two Sexes is the most faithful to the other, beares more patiently the Misfortunes that happen in Marriage; and thereby make appear greater Wisdom, and Discretion.

All the Families (for the most part) are Ruled by the Wives, to whom their Husbands resigne the Government: And the Care that therein they take of the Education of their Children, is more considerable to Families, and more important to the Common-Wealth, than that which they take of the Estate; they bequeath themselves wholly to their Good, and Wellfare: The Fear which they are in, lest any hurt should befall them, is often so great, that (many times) it robs them of their Rest: They deprive themselves often of their most necessary Enjoyments, to the end that they may want nothing: They cannot see them suffer in the least, without suffering themselves to the bottom of their Souls. And we may say, That it is their greatest pain, that they cannot ease them, by charging themselves with their Troubles.

Who can be ignorant, how earnestly they labour to instruct them in the ways of Vertue, as much as their tender Age is capable of? They endeavour to make them know and fear *God*, and teach them to Worship him in a manner suitable, and proportionate, to their Years:[49] They take care to place them in the hands of Masters, as soon as they are fit; and choose such (with all imaginable Caution) who may improve them in their Breeding: And, which is most to be esteemed, they always joyne good Example to their Instruction.

If we should descend into an intire Catalogue, and Retail of all the Occurrences of Life, and of all the Vertues which *Women* practise therein, and thereof examine the most Important Circumstances; we might have Subject enough to enlarge into a most ample Panegyrick. We might represent how far their Sobriety in Eating, and Drinking, does go; their Patience in Trouble; their Courage, and Fortitude, in supporting Affliction. Fatigues, Watchings, and Fastings; their Moderation in Pleasures, and Passions; their Inclination to do good; their Prudence in Affairs; their Integrity in all their Actions. And, in a word, we might make appear, that there is no kind of Vertue, which is not common to them with us; But, on the other hand, that there are a great many considerable Faults, which are peculiar to *Men.*

These are the general and ordinary Observations, upon what concernes *Women* in reference to the Qualities of the Mind; the Use and Practice of which, is the onely thing that ought to put a Distinction among *Men.*

Now, since there is not any Rancounter, where *Men* may not discover the Inclination, the Genius, the Vice, the Vertue, and the Capacity of Persons; those (who would undeceive themselves concerning this Subject of *Women*) have alwayes occasion to do so in Publick, or in Private; at the Court, and at the Convent; in Recreations, and Exercises; with the Poor, as well as the Rich; in whatsoever Condition, or Quality they be. And, if we consider sincerely, and without Interest, what may be observed on their behalf, we shall find, that if there be some Appearances which seem less favourable to *Women*, there are also more which are most advantagious for them; that it is not for want of Merit (but of good Luck, and Strength) that their Condition is not Equal to ours: And, in fine, that the common Opinion is but a popular, and ill-grounded Prejudice.

The Second Part

Wherein is made appear, That the Reasons which may be adduced against the Opinion of The Equality of the two Sexes, *from Poets, Oratours, Historians, Lawyers, and Philosophers; are all Idle, and Fruitless.*

*T*HAT which confirms the Vulgar in the thought which they have of *Women*, is, That they find it propt, and supported, by the Sentiment of the Learned: So that, the Publick Voice of those who Rule by Credit, agreeing in certain general Appearances, to the Disadvantage of *Women*; it is not to be wondered at, to see them so ill entertained in the Minds of the Ignorant, and Simple. And, it happens in this as in a great many other things, that *Men* confirm themselves in one Mistake, by another, Prejudice.

The Notion of Truth being Naturally pinn'd to that of Knowledge, *Men* fail not to take that for true, which is proposed to them by those who have the Reputation of being Learned: And, as the number of those which are such only by name, is far greater than of these who are so indeed; the generality of *Men* (who only count Heads) do rank themselves amongst the former; and do so much the more willingly embrace their Opinions, as they find them conformable to such as they have already entertained.

Wherefore, seeing that *Poets, Oratours, Historians* and *Philosophers*, proclaim (likewise) *Women* to be Inferiour, less

Noble, and Perfect, than *Men*, they perswade themselves thereof the more, because they are ignorant, that their Knowledg is the same Prejudice with their own (though of some-what greater extent, and more specious); and that they do no more, but joyne, to the Impression of Custom the Sentiments of the Antients; upon the Authority of whom, all their Certainty is grounded. And I find, that (in respect of their Sex) they that have studied, and they that have no Reading,[50] fall commonly into the same Mistake; which is, To judge, that whatsoever they (whom they esteem) do say, is true; because, they are already perswaded, that they say well; instead of forbearing to think that they say well, till that they are assured, that they speak nothing but what is true.

Poets and *Orators*, having no other Designe but to please and perswade; Probability and appearance of Truth, serves them to deal with the most part of *Men*: So that, Exaggerations and Hyperbolies, being most proper to that purpose, in Magnifying and Raising their Notions, according as they have need, they render Good or Evil, Small or Great, at their Pleasure: And, by a very ordinary fetch, they attribute to all *Women* in general, that which they find but in some of them in particular. It is enough to them, to have known some *Women* Hypocrites, to make them say, That the whole Sex is Guilty of that Failing. The Ornaments with which they set off their Discourse, do wonderfully contribute to gain them the Credit of such, as are not upon their Guard. They speak smoothly, and with Grace; and imploy some certain, pretty, taking (and not common) Formes of Speech; whereby they dazle the Mind, and hinder the discerning of Truth.

Men see a great many peeces (in appearance) very strong against *Women*, and yield[51] thereunto; because they know not what it is, that makes up the Force and Verity thereof; that it is only the Figures of Eloquence, Metaphors, Proverbs, Descriptions, Similitudes, Emblems, and other Flowers of *Rhetorick*:[52] And, because that there is ordinarily a good deal of Wit and Art in such kind of Works, they imagine (likewise) that there is as much of Truth.

One perswades himself, that *Women* love to hear Tales told them; because he hath (perhaps) read the Sonnet of *Sarrazin*, upon the Fall of the first *Woman*; whom he feignes only to have slipt, for lending her Ear to Flourishes of the Devil. It is true, the Fancy is pleasing, the Cast pretty, the Application proper enough to his Designe, and the Fall most Ingenious: But, if we examine the Piece to the bottom, and turn it into Prose, we shall find, that there can be nothing more false or faint.

There are some People silly enough to imagine, that *Women* are more inclined to Fury than *Men*; because they have read, that the Poets have represented the Furies under the shape of *Women*; without considering, that this is only a Poetical Fancy: And that Painters, who paint the Harpyes with the face of a *Woman*, paint likewise the Devil under the Appearance of a *Man*.

I have known[53] some undertake to prove *Women* Inconstant, from this, That a famous *Latin* Poet hath said, That they are subject to a continual Change; and that another *French Poet* hath pleasantly compared them to a Weather-Cock, which turns with the Wind; Not minding, that all these manners of speaking are onely fit to tickle, but not instruct, the Mind.

Vulgar Eloquence is a speaking Optick, which represents Objects under what shape and colour *Men* please; and there is not any Vertue, which may not be made appear Vice, by the Means which Eloquence affords.

There is nothing more ordinary, than to find among the Authors, that *Women* are not so noble or perfect as *Men*; but, for Reasons, we see none: So that, there is great likely-hood, that they have taken their Perswasions as the Vulgar do.

Women have no share with us in External Advantages, as Sciences and Authority, wherein *Men* commonly place Perfection; and therefore, they are not so perfect as we.

But, to be seriously convinced of this, it ought to be proved, That they are not thereto admitted, because they are not at all proper; but that is not so easie as *Men* conceive: Nor shall it be difficult (in the Sequel) to make the contrary appear; and that the Errour ariseth from this, That *Men* have but a confused Notion of Perfection and Nobility.

All the Arguments of those who maintain, That the lovely Sex is neither so Noble, nor Excellent as ours, are founded on this, That *Men* being the Masters, they believe that all is their own: And I am assured, that they would more strongly believe the contrary, (I mean, that the *Men* are only cut out for the *Women*) if they had all the Authority in their Hands, as in the Empire of the *Amazons*.

It is true, that here amongst us they discharge no Offices, but what are esteemed the Lowest: And, it is also true, that (upon that account) neither Religion, nor Reason, values them the less. There is nothing base and low but Vice, nor great but Vertue: And, *Women* shewing greater Vertue than *Men* (in their lesser Imployments), deserve likewise to be more esteemed. And yet, I know not, whether (in regard of their ordinary Charge, which is to Nurse and Bring-up their Children) they are not worthy of the first Place in Civil Society.

Were we free, and without Common-Wealth, we would not assemble our selves together; but for the better Preservation of Life, in the peaceable Enjoyment of those things which are necessary thereto; and would have greater Esteem for those who should hereunto contribute in greatest measure.

It is by reason of this, that we are accustomed to look on our Prince, as the chief Person of the State; because his Care and Fore-sight is the most general, and of greatest Extent; and, by Proportion, we Respect those that are under him. Most part of *Men* preferr Souldiers to Judges, because they directly oppose themselves to those who (in most terrible manner) attack our Lives; and every one sets a Value upon Persons, as they judge them more or less useful. So that, *Women* seem to be the most Estimable, since their Service (which they render to the Publick) is incomparably greater than that of all others whosoever.

Men might absolutely dispense with Princes, Souldiers, and Merchants, as they did in the beginning of the World;

and as Savages do still, even to this Day: But, in our Infancy, we cannot be without *Women*. In states that are well pacified, the most part of those who have Authority, are as *Men* dead and useless; but *Women* never cease to be necessary to us. The Ministers of Justice are only proper to preserve Goods and Estates,[54] to those who possess them; but *Women*, to preserve Life. Souldiers are employed for *Men*, grown up, and capable to defend themselves; but *Women* labour for *Men*, when as yet they know not what they are, if they have Enemies, or Friends; and at that time, when they have no other Arms but Tears, against such as attack them. Masters, Magistrates, and Princes, do not often-times bestir themselves, but for Glory, and particular Interest; when *Women* do nothing but for the good of the Children, whom they breed. In short, The Pains, the Cares, the Troubles, and Assiduities, to which they expose themselves, can in no wise be matched in any other state (of Civil Society) whatsoever.

There is nothing (then) but Fancy, which renders them less Valuable. *Men* would largely Reward him who had tamed a Tyger: Such who have the Skill to train Horses, Apes, and Elephants, are well considered of; and we speak, with Elogy, of a *Man* that hath composed a small Work which hath cost him but little time and pains; And shall we neglect *Women*: that spend many Years in breeding and forming of Children? If we enquire into the Reason thereof, we shall find, it is, Because the one is (onely) more ordinary than the other.

What *Historians* say to the Prejudice of *Women*, makes deeper Impression on the Minds of *Men*, than the Discourses of *Orators*; For, as they seem to put forth nothing of their own Heads, so is their Testimony less suspected: Besides, that it is suitable to that whereof *Men* are already perswaded, when they report *Women* to have been in former times, the same which they are believed to be at present. But all the Authority which they have upon the spirits of *Men*, is nothing but a very common Prejudice, in regard of Antiquity; which *Men* represent to themselves, under the Image of a Venerable Old *Man*, who (having much Wisdom and Experience) is uncapable of being deceived, or of speaking any thing but Truth.

Whil'st, in the mean time, the Antients are no less *Men* than we are, and as much subject to Errour; and we ought no more at present to assent to their Opinions, than we would have done in their own times. *Men* heretofore considered *Women* as now they do, and with as little Reason: So, whatsoever *Men* say concerning that, ought to be suspected; seeing they are both Judge and Party. And when any one brings against them the Sentiments of a thousand Authors, that History is only to be considered, as a Tradition of Prejudices and Mistakes. There is, also, as little Fidelity and Exactitude in Antient *Histories,* as there is in Familiar Rehearsals; wherein we sufficiently know, that there is (almost) none at all. They that have wrote *Them,* have there-with mingled their Passions and Interest; and the most part (having but had confused Notions of Vice and Vertue) have often mistaken the one for the other. And those, who like-wise Read *Them* (with the ordinary Pre-occupation) fail not to run into the same Fault.

In the Prejudice wherein they have been engaged, they have made it their business, to exaggerate and raise the Vertues, and Advantages, of their own Sex; and to debase and weaken the Merit of *Women,* by a contrary Interest: This is so easie to be discovered, that I need not adduce Instances.

Notwithstanding, if we can but a little rip-up what is past, we may find enought to prove, that *Women* have not in any thing yielded to men; and that the Vertue which they have made appear, hath been more excellent: if we sincerely consider all the Circumstances thereof, we may observe, that they have giv'n as great markes of Wit, and Capacity, upon all occasions; That there have beem some who have governed great States and Empires with Wisdom, and moderation, that cannot be parallel'd: others who have rendred Justice with an integrity equall to that of the *Athenian Areopagites*; Many, who by their prudence, and councells, have restablished peace, and tranquility to Kingdomes, and a throne to their Husbands. Some have been seen at the head of Armies, or with a courage more than *Heroical* defending themselves upon the walls of Townes. How many have there been, whose Chastity could receive no blemish, neither by the terrible threats, nor splendid promises which men made to them, and who with a Generous, and astonishing Gallantry, have endured the most horrible torments, for the cause of Religion! How many have there been, who have rendered themselves as compleat as men in all sorts of Sciences! who have dived into the most Curious Secrets of Nature, the most quaint of Policy, the most solid of Morality, and who have Elevated themselves to the highest Pitch of Christian Divinity! So that History, which the prejudiced abuse against that Sex to abase it, may serve to those who look thereon with the eyes of equity, to prove that it is in all respects as noble as our own.

The Authority of Laws has a great Weight upon many men, as to that which concerns the *Women*, because they make particular profession of rendering to every one their right. They place the Wives under the Jurisdiction of their Husbands, as children under the power of their fathers; and alledge, that it is Nature that hath so assigned them the smaller functions of Society, and placed them at distance from publick Authority.

Men think themselves sufficiently grounded to say the same after them: but I hope it is lawfull without wounding the Respect which is their due, to differ from them in Judgement. We should strangely puzzle them, If we obliged them to explain themselves intelligibly about that which they call Nature in this case, and make us understand in what manner she hath distinguished the two Sexes, as they pretend.

We must consider that they who have made or compiled the Law, being men, have favoured their own Sex, as *Women* possibly might have done had they been in their place: And Laws being made since the Constitution of Societies, in the same manner in respect of *Women* as they are at present; the Lawyers who had likewise their prejudice, have attributed to Nature a distinction, which is only drawing from Custome, besides that it was not at all necessary to change the order which they found setled, for obtaining the end that they proposed, which was the good government of a State by the administration of justice. To be short, if they should be headstrong, to hold, that *Women* are naturally in a condition of dependance upon men, we might fight them with their own weapons, since they themselves acknowledge dependance, and servitude, to be contrary to the order of Nature, which renders all mankind equal.

Dependence being a meer Corporal, and Civil Relation, ought not to be considered but as an effect of chance, force, or custome; except in the case of Children to those who have given them life. And yet neither does that pass a certain age, wherein men being supposed to have reason, and experience enough to guide themselves, are freed by the Lawes, from the authority of an other.

Amongst persons of an equal or not much different age, there only ought to be a reasonable subordination, according to which those who have less understanding, willingly submit themselves to such as have more. And if we remove the Civil Priviledges, which the Laws have bestowed on men, and which establish them heads of the family; we cannot find betwixt them, and their wives, any other submission but that of Experience, and Knowledge: both one, and other freely engage themselves at the same time, when the Wives have as much,[55] and often more Judgement than the Husbands. Their Promises and Covenants of Marriage are reciprocal; and the power equal upon one and others Body; And if the Lawes give the Husband more Authority over the estate, Nature allowes the Wife more power, and right, over the Children. And as the will of the one is not the Rule of the other; if the wife be obliged to do what the Husband minds her of, he is no less bound to follow the advertisements of the Wife, when she tells him his duty: And, except it be in matters just, and reasonable, the Wife is not to be constrained to submit her self to the pleasure of her Husband, unless you'l say that he is stronger; which is the dealing of a *Turk* with a *Moore*, and not of *Men* of reason.[56]

We shall not need much trouble to rid our selves of the opinion of the Learned, of whom I have spoken: because we may easily be satisfied that their profession does not engage them to so exact an enquiry into the nature of things; Appearances, and probabilities, are sufficient for Poets and Orators; The Testimony of Antiquity to Historians; And Custome and Practice to Lawyers, to bring them to their intended end: But as to the Sentiment of *Philosophers*, we must not so easily pass it; seeing that they seem to be above all the preceding considerations, as indeed they ought to be; and that they are thought to try matters more strictly; which gaines them the common credit, and makes it believed unquestionable what they assert, especially when they contradict not the received opinions.

So the Common People confirm themselves in the opinion, that there is inequality betwixt the two Sexes, because they see those whose Judgements they regard as the measures of their own, and the same opinion; not knowing that the most part of *Philosophers* walk by no other Rule than that of the Vulgar, and that it is not by Vertue of Science or Knowledge, that they often dictate especially concerning the matter in hand. They have carryed their prejudices even to the Schools, where they have learned nothing that might serve to disengage them there-from: On the contrary, all their Science is founded upon the Judgements that they have made from their Cradle; And with them it is a crime or Errour to call in question that which they believed before the years of discretion. They are not taught to know *Man* by the body, nor by the soul: And that which they teach, commonly may very well serve to prove, that betwixt us, and beasts, there is no difference, but that of Lesser and Greater in the Same kind. They hear not a word of Sexes: They are supposed to know them sufficiently already; Very far from Examining the Capacity, and real and natural difference, betwixt them; which is one of the most curious, and probably also the most important Question of all natural or Moral *Philosophy*. They spend whole years, and some all their lives, at Trifles, and *Entia Rationis*, being no where to be found without their own Brains;[57] and to plod and find-out, whether or not, there be beyond the world imaginary Spaces; and whether the atoms or small dust which appeares in the Beams of the Sun, may be sliced out into infinite parts. What solid ground can we lay upon, what the learned of this kind say, when we are to treat of serious, and important matters?

Men may think, nevertheless, that (though they be so ill taught themselves, yet) their Principles (probably) are sufficient to discover, which of the two Sexes have (naturally) the advantage of the other; But none can think so, but such who either know them not, or are pre-possessed thereby. The Knowledge of our selves, is absolutely necessary to enable us, for the handling of that Question aright; and especially, the knowledge of our Body, which is the Organ of Sciences; after the same manner, as for to know how Telescopes, and Glasses of Approach, magnifie the Objects: we must know the Fashion of them. They touch not this but in passing, no more than they do Truth, and Science; I mean, the Method of acquiring true and certain Knowledges; without which, it is impossible to examine, Whether or not *Women* be as capable thereof, as our selves? And, without amusing my self to repeat the Notions that they give us thereon, I shall declare (in general) what my Thoughts are thereof.

All Man-kind being made alike, have the same Sentiments, and Notions, of Natural things; for example, of Light, Heat, and Hardness; And all the Knowledge which we labour to gain there-from, is reduced to this, That we may truly find out what is the Disposition (internal and external) of every Object, which produceth in us the thoughts, and conceits, which we have of them. All that Masters can do, to guide us to this Knowledge, is but, So to apply our Minds to what we remark, that we may examine the Appearances and Effects thereof, without Precipitation or Prejudice; and to shew us the Order, which we are to observe in the ranking of our Thoughts, for to find what we look for.

For instance, If an Illiterate Person should desire me to explain to him, Wherein consists the Liquidity of Water; I would not assert any thing, but only ask him, What he had observed thereof? How, that if Water be not contained in a Vessel, it sheds? that is to say, that all the Parts thereof separate and dis-unite of themselves, without the Intermixtion of any other Body; that we may thrust there into our Fingers without trouble, and without finding Resistance as from harder Bodies? And that, in putting therein, Sugar or Salt, we perceive, that these two Bodies dissolve, piece and piece; and that all the Parcels thereof are dispersed through the several parts of the Liquor.

Hitherto, I should teach him no new thing; And if (after the same manner) I had told him, What it is to be in Repose, or in Motion; I should have brought him to acknowledge, that the Nature of Liquors consists[58] in this, That their insensible Particles are in perpetual Motion; which requires them to be enclosed in a Vessel, and disposes them to give easie Entry to hard Bodies: And that the Particles of Water, which are little, glib, and pointed, (insinuating themselves into the Pores of the Sugar) shake and divide the Parts thereof, by their Justling; and, moving themselves every way, transport with them into all the Quarters of the Vessel, that which they have separated.

This Notion of Liquors (which is a Part, taken from the Body of Natural *Philosophy*) would appear a great deal more clear, if we saw it in its proper Place and Order: and it hath nothing, which the meanest sort of *Women* are not able to understand. The rest of all our Knowledges (being proposed in Order and Method) have no greater Difficulty: And if we consider attentively, we shall find, that every Science of Reasoning, requires but less wit and time, than is necessary to learn to make Point or Tapistry.

In effect, the Notions of Natural things are necessary, and we form them alwayes after the same manner: *Adam* had them as we have; *Children* have them as Old *Men*, and *Women* as *Men*: And these *Idea*'s are renewed, confirmed, and entertained, by the continual use of Sense. The Mind is alwayes in Action; and he that knows well how it proceeds in one thing, discovers (without trouble) how it works in all others. There is nothing (but More and Less) betwixt the Impression made by the *Sun*, and that of a Spark of *Fire*: And, to think well thereon, there is neither need of great Skill, nor Exercise of Body.

It is not so, in the Works of which I have spoken. There is need of greater Application of Spirit; the *Idea*'s thereof being Arbitrary, are harder to be learned, and retained; which is the cause, that so much time is necessary for to Learn (well) a Trade, because it depends on long Exercise. There is Skill required, rightly to observe the Proportions on a Canvas; to Distribute equally the Silk or the Wool; to mingle with Exactness the Colours; neither to joyne too close, nor keep too open, the Points; to place no more in one Rank, than in another; to make the little Knots[59] imperceptible. In a word, One must know to make and vary, in a thousand different Wayes the Works of Art, to be skillful therein; when, as in Sciences, there is no more required, but an orderly viewing of Works already made, and alwayes Uniform: and, all the difficulty of Success therein, proceeds more from the Incapacity of Masters, than from the Objects, or Disposition of the Body.

We must not then (any more) wonder to see *Men* and *Women*, (without Study) entertain themselves, about things which concern Sciences; since the Method of Teaching of them, serves only to certifie our Judgements, which are confounded by Precipitation, Custom, and Use.

The Notion which we have given of Knowledge (in general) might suffice to perswade unprejudiced Persons, That *Men* and *Women* are equally capable thereof; But, because the contrary Opinion is most deeply rooted, we must (for the intire plucking of it up) Fight it by Principles; to the end, that (joyning the Appearances, agreeing to the Beautiful Sex, which have been presented in the First Part, with the Natural Reasons which we shall here-after adduce) *Men* may fully be convinced, in favour of it.

That **Women** *(considered according to the Principles of Sound* **Philosophy***) are as capable as* **Men,** *of all Sorts of Sciences.*

It is easie to be Remarked, That the Difference of Sexes, regards only the Body: there being no other, but that Part (properly) which serves for the Production of *Men*: And, the Spirit concurring no other way but by its Consent (which it lends to all after the same manner) we may conclude, That in it there is not Sex at all.

If we consider it in our selves, we find it equal, and of the same Nature in all *Men*, and capable of all sorts of Thoughts; The smallest busie it as well as the greatest; and there is no less required to the right knowing of a *Gnat*,[60] than of an *Elephant*: Whosoever knows wherein consists the Light (and Fire) of a Sparkle, knows also, the Light of the *Sun*. When we are accustomed to reflect on things which only concern the Spirit, we perceive therein all (at least) as clearly, as in the most material things which are discerned by the senses. I can discover no greater difference between the Spirit of a dull, and ignorant man, and that of that one who is delicate, and ingenious, than betwixt the Spirit of the same man considered at the age of ten years, and at the age of Fourty: And since there appeareth no more betwixt that of the two Sexes, we may affirm, that their difference is not on that side, the constitution of the body; But particularly the Education, Exercise, and the impressions that come from all that does surround us, being every where the Natural, and Sensible causes of so many diversities as are observed therein.

It is God who unites the Soul to the Body of a *Woman*, as to that of a *Man*, and who joynes them by the same Lawes. The sentiments, the passions, and inclinations, make and entertain that Union; And the Spirit operating after the same manner in the one as well as the other, is there equally capable of the same things.

This is yet more clear, when we consider onely the Head, the sole organe of Sciences, and where the soul exerciseth all its functions; the most exact Anatomy remarks to us no difference in this part between *Men*, and *Women*, their brain is altogether like to ours: The impressions of sense are received, and muster themselves there in the same fashion, and are no otherwise preserved for Imagination, and Memory. *Women* hear, as we do, by the ears; they see by the eyes; and they tast with the Tongue; And there is nothing peculiar in the disposition of these Organs, but that the *Women* have them ordinarily more delicate, which is an advantage. So that the outward objects affect[61] them after the same manner, Light by the eyes, and Sound by the eares. Who can hinder them then to apply themselves to the consideration of themselves? To Examine in what consists the nature of the soul; how many kinds of thoughts there are, and how they are excited by occasion of certain corporeal Motions; to consult afterwards the natural Notions, which they have of God; and to begin with things Spiritual to dispose in order their thoughts, and to frame to themselves that Science which we call, the *Metaphysicks*?

Since they have also eyes, and hands, may they not make themselves, or see others perform, the dissection of an humane body? consider the Symmetry, and structure thereof; observe the diversity, difference, and relation of its parts: their figures, their motion, and functions; the Alterations to which they are Subject? and to conclude, on the means to preserve them in good disposition, and to restore it to them, when it is changed.

They need no more for this, but to know the nature of Extrinsical bodies, which have any reference to their own, discover their Properties, and all that renders them capable of making any impression good or bad thereon; this is known by the aid of the Senses, and by the various Experiments that are made upon them: And *Women* being equally capable of the one as well as the other, might learn as well as we, *Physick* and Medicine.

Is there need of so much understanding, to know, that Breathing is absolutely necessary for the preservation of life; and that it is performed by the means of the Air, which entering by the pipe of the nose and mouth, is insinuated into the lungs, for the cooling of the blood which passeth that way in Circulation, and there causeth different Alterations, according as it is more or less Gross by the Mixture of Vapours, and Exhortations, with which we see it sometimes blended.

Is it a matter so difficult to discover, that the tast of Food consists on the part of the body (in the different manner how it is allayed on the tongue) by the Spitle? There is no Person, but finds after meals, that the Victuals which then are put into the mouth, being divided quite otherways than those with which we are Nourished, cause there a Sensation less pleasing. That which remains to be known of the Functions of Mans body, being considered in order, have nothing more of difficulty.

The Passions are certainly that which is most Curious in this matter: We may therein observe two things, the Motions of the body, with the thoughts and stirrings of the Soul, which concurr in them. *Women* may know this, as easily as we do. And as to the causes which excite Passions, we know how they do it, When we have once by the study of Natural Philosophy comprehended their manner, how Circumambient things affect and touch us; And by experience, and use, how we thereto apply, or separate, our wills and inclinations.

In making regular Meditations upon the objects of the three Sciences lastly spoken of, a *Woman* may observe, that the order of her thoughts ought to follow that of Nature; that then they are exact when they[62] conform thereto; that there is nothing but hast, and precipitation in our Judgements, which hinders that exactitude. And marking consequentially the Oeconomy which she hath observed to attain thereto, she may make Reflections, which may serve her as a Rule for the future, and form to her-self there-from a Logick.

If it be objected notwithstanding of this, That *Women* by themselves could never acquire these knowledges, (which is said); at least we cannot deny, but that with the help of Masters, and Books, they might; As the ablest men in all ages have done.

It is enough to alledge the acknowledged property of the Sex, to prove it capable of understanding the proportions of the Mathematicks: And we should contradict our selves to doubt, that if it applyed it self to the making of Engines, it would succeed as well therein as our own; since we our selves allow it more invention and artifice.

There is need but of eyes, and a little attention, in observing the Appearances of nature, To make us remark that the Sun, and all the Luminous bodyes of the Heavens, are real Fires, since they heat, and light us, in the same manner as the Fires here below; that they appear'd successively to answer to several parts of the earth, and so be able to judge of their Motion and Course: And whosoever can roul in his head great designs, and set to work the Movements thereof, may there likewise with exactness turn the whole Machin of the World, if he have but once well observed the diverse Appearances of the same.

We have already found in *Women*, all the Dispositions which render *Men* proper for the Sciences, which concern them (separately) in themselves: And, if we continue to consider them within distance, we shall also find in them those which are necessary for the Sciences, which regard them, as tyed altogether with their like in Civil Society.

It is a Fault in *Vulgar Philosophy*, to place amongst Sciences so great a Distinction; that, following that peculiar Method of it, we cannot acknowledge any Tye or Coherence amongst them: which is the cause, that we restrain so much the Extent of Humane Understanding; imagining to our selves, that the same *Man* is never (almost) capable of many Sciences; that, to be fit for *Natural Phylosophy* or *Medicine*, one is not thereby proper for *Rhetorick* or *Divinity*: and that there ought to be as many different Capacities, as there are Sciences, in the World.[63]

This Thought proceeds on the one hand, from this, That *Men* confound (ordinarily) Nature with Custome; in taking the Disposition of certain Persons to one Science, rather than another, for an Effect of their Natural Constitution; when indeed, it is often but a Casual Inclination, coming from Necessity, Education, or Habit: And, on the other hand, for want of having Remarked, that there is (properly) but one Science in the World, which is the Knowledge of our selves; and, that all others are onely particular Applications thereof.

In effect, the Difficulty which we find at this day to learn the Tongues, Moral Philosophy, and the rest; consists only in this, That we know not how to referr them to this general Science: From whence, it may have arrived, That all those who have believed *Women* capable of *Natural Philosophy* and *Medicine*, may not have therefore judged them capable of the Sciences that we are to speak of. However, the Difficulty is the same on both sides: It is the business in All, to think aright: And this we do, by applying seriously our Minds, to the Objects which represent themselves to us; that we may raise from them clear and distinct Notions; that we may eye them in all their different Faces and Relations; and that we may pass no Judgement thereon, but upon what appears manifestly true. With this we need no more, but to dispose our Thoughts in a Natural Order, for the obtaining of a perfect Science: And here, there is nothing too High for *Women*; For, such of them who may be (by this way) instructed in *Natural Philosophy* and *Medicine*, may likewise (by the same) become capable of all others.

Wherefore, might they not perceive, that the necessity of living in Society, obliging us to Communicate our Thoughts by some External Signes; the most expedient of all others, is Speech; which consists in the use of Words, agreed on amongst *Men*, That we ought to have as many of them, as we have Notions of things? That they ought to have some Relation of Sound and Signification one with another, to make us learn and retain them with more ease, and that we should not be forced to multiply them infinitely? That they must be Marshalled in the Order most natural, and suitable, to our Thoughts; and that we should not employ more in Discourse, than what may be enough to make us be understood?

These Reflexions might put a *Woman* in Condition, to labour (like a Virtuosi) for the perfecting of her Mother-Tongue;[64] by reforming, and cutting off the bad Words, introducing of New, Regulating Custom by Reason, and the true Notions which we have of Languages: And the Method, by which she might have Learned the Language of her Country, would wonderfully help her to the attaining of that of Strangers, to discover the Delicacies thereof, to read Authors, and to become most exact in *Grammar*, and that which is called *Humanity*.

Women (as well as *Men*) Discourse of things, to make them be understood, in the same manner, as they know them; and to dispose others to do as they would have them, which is called Perswading: In this they Naturally succeed better than we. And yet, to perform it still with Art, they have no more to do, but to study to represent things, as they present themselves to them; or as they would represent them to themselves, if they were in the Place of those whom they would affect.

All *Men* (being made after the same manner) are (almost) alwayes moved in like manner by Objects; And, if there be any Difference, it proceeds from their Inclinations, their Habits, or their Quality; which a *Woman* might know with a little Reflexion, and Custom: And, being able to dispose her Thoughts in the manner most convenient, express them neatly, and with Grace; adding thereto, the Gestures, the Air of the Countenance, and the Voice, she might become Mistress of the most perfect Eloquence.

It is not credible, that *Women* can so highly practise Vertue, without being able to penetrate into the Fundamental Maxims thereof: In effect, a *Woman* already so instructed as we above represented her, might discover of her self the Measures of her Conduct, by discovering the three kinds of Duties which comprehend all Morality; of which, the first regards *God*, the second our Selves, and the third our Neighbour. The clear and distinct Notions, which she may have formed of her Spirit, and the Union thereof with the Body, must (infallibly) lead her to acknowledge, That there is another Spirit Infinite, the Author of all Nature; and to entertain of Him the Sentiments, upon which Religion is founded. And after, having (by *Natural Philosophy*) learned wherein it is, that Sensual Pleasure does consist, and in what manner External Things contribute to the Perfection of the Mind, and the Preservation of the Body; she cannot fail to conclude, That we must be great Enemies to our selves, if we use them not with great Moderation. And, if she come, in Sequel, to consider her Self, as engaged in Civil Society, with others of the same Nature, subject to the same Passions, and to the necessities (which can not be satisfied without mutual assistance); she must without trouble fall upon this thought upon which depends all our Justice, That we ought to do to others as we would be done to; and, that we ought to bridle those desires, whereof the exorbitancy which is called Lusting or Covetousness,[65] occasions all the trouble, and all the unhappiness of life.

She might the more still confirm her self in the perswasion of the last of these duties, if she advanced, and carried on her thoughts, to the point of discovering the ground of Policy, and of Law and Justice. And, as both the one and other, only regard the duties of men amongst themselves, she would judge, that, Fully to comprehend to what it is that they are obliged in civil Society, we must understand what it is that hath inclined men to establish it. She would then consider them as out of any such Society, and find them all intirely free, and equal, with the desire only to preserve themselves, and a right alike to all upon every thing that might be necessary thereto. But she finding that this equality engageth men in warr, or continual mistrust (a thing contrary to their end) the light of nature would dictate, that they could not live in peace, without that every one yeelded somewhat of his right, and came to covenants, and contracts: And that to render these Actions valid, and stop all Jealousy, it would be necessary to have recourse to a third person, who taking upon him Authority, might force everyone to perform what they had promised to others; That he being chosen only for the good of his subjects, ought to have no other designe; And that to obtain the end of this institution, it is necessary he should be the Master of Lives, and Estates; of Peace and of Warr.

In Examining this matter, and the depth, what would hinder a Woman that she should not discover, What natural equity is; What are Contract, Authority, and Obedience; what is the nature of Law, the use of Penalties; wherein consist the civil law, and that of Nations; what are the duties of Princes, and of Subjects: And in a word, by her proper Reflexions, and by Books, she might learn all that is necessary to make a Lawyer and a States-man.

After that, she may have obtained a perfect knowledge of her self, and be solidly instructed in the general rules of the conduct of Men, Probably she would become curious to inform her self also how it is that men live in strange Countreys. And as she had observed, that the changes of weather, of seasons, of place, of age, of dyet, company, and exercises, had occasioned in her, alterations and different passions, she needed not much trouble to find that these diversities produce the same effect in regard of whole nations: That they have Inclinations, Customs, Manners, and Laws different according as they are more near, or distant from Seas, the South or North, according as their countrey is plain or mountainous, watered with Rivers, and Woody, the soil more or less fruitfull, the particular kind of Food which it bringeth forth; And according to Commerce, and the affairs which they have with other Neighbouring or remote people: shee might study all these things, and so learn what are the Manners, the Riches, the Religion, the Government, and the Interests of twenty or thirty different Nations, as easily as of so many private families. For what concernes the Situation of Kingdomes, how Seas to Lands, Isles to the Continent do answer; there is no more difficulty to learn it in a Mapp, than to know the several quarters and streets of a Town; or the highwayes of the countrey, where one liveth.

The Knowledge of the present, might breed in her desire also to know what is past: And that which she may have retained of Geography, would afford her great assistance in this Designe, enabling her better to understand affairs, as Warrs, Voyages, and Negotiations,[66] marking to her the places where they have hapned; the Passages, Roads, and the boundings of States. But the skill which she may have obtained of the Transactions of men in general, by the reflections which she may have made upon her self, would bring her into the Mystery of Policy, Interest and Passions; and help her to discover the moving wheele, and spring, of enterprizes, the fountain and source of revolutions, and to supply in great Undertakings the lesser things which have made them prosper, and which have escaped Histories:[67] And following their true Notions, which she hath of Vice, and Vertue; she may observe the flattery, passion, and ignorance of Authors; and to guard her self from the Corruption, which infect men in reading of Histories, where these faults are commonly mingled. As the ancient policy, was not so refined as the modern, and the interest of Princes less conjoyned in former times than at present, and commerce of less extent; there is more Judgement required to understand, and disentangle our Gazets, than Lives of *Quintus Curtius.*[68]

There are a great many persons that find the *Ecclesiastick History* more pleasing and solid, than civil or prophane: because, there they find the effects of Reason, and Vertue, farther pursued, and that passions, and prejudices covered with a pretext of Religion, sets the mind upon a method, altogether particular in its conduct. A Woman would apply her self thereto with so much more affection, as she judged it more important. She might convince her self, that the books of *Scripture*, are as authentick, as all the others which we have; that they containe the true Religion, and all the Maxims whereon it is founded; that the *New Testament* where the History of Christianity properly begins, is no more difficult to be understood, than *Greek* and *Latin Authors*; that they that read it with the simplicity of Children, seeking only the Kingdome of God, discover the truth, and meaning thereof with more ease and pleasure, than that of ridles, emblems, and fables; And after having regulated her mind by the Morality of *Jesus Christ*, she may find her self in condition to direct others; remove their scruples, and to resolve Cases of conscience, with more solidity than if she had filled her head with all the Casuits in the world.

I see nothing that could hinder, but that in the progress of their studies, she might observe as well as a man, How it is that the Gospel hath passed from hand to hand, from Kingdom to Kingdom, from age to age, even to her own times, but that she might gain, by reading of the Fathers, the Notion of true Theology, and find out that it only consists in the Knowledge of the History of Christians; and the Particular Sentiments of those that have written thereon. So, she might render her self able to compose Works of Religion, Preach the Truth, and batter down Novelties, by shewing what hath been alwayes Believed through the whole Church, about the Matters in Controversie.

If a *Woman* be capable to inform her self from *History*, of the Nature of all Publick Societies, how they have been formed, and how they are preserved by virtue of a fixed and constant Authority, exercised by Magistrates and Officers, subordinate to one another; she is no less, to Learn the Application of that Authority, by Laws, Ordinations, and Constitutions, for the Conduct of those who are submitted thereunto, as well to the Relation of Persons (according to their several Conditions) as for the Possession and Enjoyment of Goods. Is it a thing so difficult, to know the Relation between a Husband and his Wife, between a Father and his Children, the Master and his Servants, the Land-Lord and his Tenants, betwixt those who are Allied in Affinity, betwixt a Guardian and his Pupil? Is it so great a Mystery, to understand what it is to possess by Purchase, Exchange, Donation, Legacy, Testament, Prescription, and Usufruit? and what are the necessary Conditions to render Use and Possession valid?

There appears to be no more Understanding requisite to know (aright) the spirit of Christian Society, than that of the Civil; to frame a right Notion of the Authority which is peculiar thereto, and upon which is founded all its Conduct; and to distinguish (precisely) betwixt that which *Jesus Christ* hath left to his Church, and the Dominion which onely belongs to Temporal Powers.

After having made that Distinction absolutely necessary to the right Understanding of the Canon Law, a *Woman* might study, and observe how the Church is Governed in the State; and how the Spiritual Jurisdiction is mingled with the Secular; wherein the Hierarchy consists; what are the Offices of Prelates, the Power of the Councels, Popes, Bishops, and Pastors; what is the meaning of Discipline; what are the Rules and Changes thereof; what mean Canons, Priviledges, and Exemptions; how Benefices are Established, and what is the Right and Possession thereof. In a word, What are the

Customs and Ordinances of the Church, and the Duties of all those that Compose it. There is (therein) nothing at all, whereof a *Woman* is not most capable; and so, she might become most Skilful in the Canon-Law.

These are some general Notions of the Highest Knowledges, where-with *Men* serve themselves, to signalize their Parts, and raise their Fortune; and of which, to the Prejudice of *Women*, they have been so long in Possession: And, although they have as great right thereto as themselves, *Men* (notwithstanding), entertain such Thoughts, and carry with a Conduct towards them, by so much the more unjust, that nothing like is to be seen in the use of the Goods of the Body.

It hath been judged expedient; that, for the Peace and security of Families, Prescription should take place: my Meaning is, That a *Man*, who (with a good Conscience, and without trouble or molestation) might have enjoyed the Goods of another for a certain space of time, should remain Possessour thereof, without the After-claims and Pretensions of any whosover. But, it hath never entered into the minds of *Men*, to believe, That such who had fallen from their Possessions by Neglect or otherwise; would be incapable by some manner or other, to retrive them; and their Incapacity hath never been considered as Natural, but onely Civill.

On the contrary, *Men* have not onely contented themselves not to call *Women* to a share in Sciences, and Offices, after a long Prescription against them; but have proceeded farther, to fancy, that their Exclusion therefrom, is founded on a natural Indisposition on their Part.

In the mean-while, there is nothing in the World more Fanatical than that Imagination: For, whether that we consider the Sciences in themselves, or that we regard the Organ, which serves[69] to acquire them; we shall find, that both Sexes are thereto equally disposed. There is but one only way to insinuate Truth into the Mind (whereof it is the Food), as there is but one to convey Nourishment into all sorts of Stomacks, for the Subsistance of the Body: And, as to what concerns the different Dispositions of that Organ, which renders us more or less fit for Sciences; if we would fairly and honestly acknowledge, Who have the better, we must confess it to be the *Women*.

We cannot disagree; but, amongst *Men*, such as are gross and material, are commonly stupid; and, on the other hand, the more Delicate, always most Sprightly.[70] I find the Experience of this too universal and constant, to stand in need (in this place) of the Support of Reasons: So, the lovely Sex, being of a Temperature more Fine and Delicate than ours, would not fail (at least) to match ours, if it applyed it self to Study.

I well fore-see, that this Opinion will not be relished by many; who will find it a little strange: I cannot help that. *Men* think that it concernes the Honour of our Sex to take the Place in All; And I believe it to be Justice, to render to every one that which is their right.

In effect, we All (both *Men* and *Women*) have the same Right to Truth, since the Mind in all of us is alike capable to know it; and that we are (All) affected in the same manner, by the Objects that make Impression upon the Body. This Title to Knowledges (which Nature bestows on All) springs from this, That we have All need of them, the one as well as the other. There is no Person that seeks not to be happy; It is to that, that all our Actions tend; and no Body can be solidly so, but by clear and distinct Knowledges: For, it is in that, that *Jesus Christ* himself, and St. *Paul*, make us believe, will consist the Happiness of the other Life. A Covetous Man never esteems himself happy, but when he knows that he possesses great Riches: An Ambitious Person, when he perceives that he is above others. In a word, All the Happiness of *Men* (Real or Imaginary) is only placed in Knowledge; that is to say, In the Thought which they have, that they possess the Good which they desire.

It is this which makes me believe, that there is nothing but the Notions of Truth (which we procure by Study, and which are fixt and independant from the Possession or Want of things), that can make up the true Happiness of this Life. For, that which makes that a Covetous Man cannot be happy in the simple Knowledge of Riches, is; Because that, that

Knowledge which renders him happy, ought to be joyned with the Enjoyment, or the Imagination of possessing of them for the present: And, when his Imagination presents them to him as distant from him, and out of his Power, he cannot reflect thereon without being afflicted.

It is altogether otherwise with the Knowledge which we have of our Selves, and of all those which depend thereon; but, particularly, of those which enter into the Society of Life. Since then, that both Sexes are capable of the same Felicity, they have Equall Right to all that which conduceth to the obtaining thereof.

When we say, That Happiness consists (chiefly) in the Knowledge of Truth, we exclude not Vertue; On the contrary, we think that it maketh up the most Essential Part thereof: Yet, a *Man* is not happy by Vertue, but in so much as he knoweth that he enjoyes it, or that he endeavours so to do; that is to say, That although it be sufficient to make a *Man* esteemed happy, that we see him practice Vertue (though he know it not perfectly); and also, that such a Practice (with a confused and imperfect Knowledge) may contribute to purchase the Happiness of the other Life:[71] yet, it is certain, that he cannot esteem himself solidly happy, without he be Conscious to himself that he does good; as he would not at all believe himself Rich, without he possessed Wealth.

The Reason why there are so few that have a Relish of, or Love for, true Vertue, is, Because they know it not; and, not at all minding when they practice it, they feel not that Satisfaction which it produceth, and which makes up that Felicity of which we speak. That ariseth from this, That Vertue is not a simple Speculation of Good, to which we are obliged; but an Effective Desire, which springs from the Perswasion that we have thereof: And we cannot practice it with Delight, without the Resentment of some Emotion; because it happens with it, as with the most Excellent Liquors, that seem some-time bitter, or without Sweetness; if, when they are upon the Tongue, the Mind be other-wise taken up, and does not apply it self to the Alterations which there they cause.

The two Sexes have not only need of Light, to find their Happiness in the Practice of Vertue; but likewise, need thereof to practise aright. It is Perswasion that sets us at work; and we are so much the more perswaded of our Duty, as the more perfectly we know it.

That little which we have said here concerning Morality, sufficeth to insinuate, that the Knowledge of our selves, is most important to strengthen the Perswasion of the Duties, to which we are obliged. And it would not be difficult to shew, how all others contribute thereto; nor to make appear, that the Reason why so many Persons practise Vertue so ill, or fall into Looseness, is only the Ignorance of themselves, and what they are.

The Reason why People commonly believe, That *Men* need not be knowing for to become Vertuous, is, Because we see many vitious Persons, that otherwise pass for Intelligent; from whence, they imagine, that Knowledge is not only unprofitable for Vertue, but even that it is many times destructive thereto. And, this Errour renders the most part of those who have the Reputation of being more Witty than others, suspect to weak Judgements; and, at the same time, makes them slight, and be averse, from the Highest Knowledges.

Men take no notice, that there is nothing but false Lights, which cast and leave *Men* in Disorder; because that the confused Notions (which false *Philosophy* gives us of our Selves, and of that which makes up the Body of our Actions), so bemists the Mind,[72] that not knowing it self, nor the Nature of the things which surround it, nor the Relation which they have to its self; and not being able to bear the weight of Difficulties which present themselves in that obscurity: it must necessarily succumb, and abandon it self to its Passions; Reason being too weak to stop it.

It is (then) but a *Panick Fear*, which hath given occasion to the Capricious Imagination[73] of the Vulgar, That Study and Learning would render *Women* more Wicked and Proud: There is nothing but false Knowledge, capable to produce so bad an Effect. A *Woman* cannot Learn[74] true Knowledge, without becoming thereby more Humble and Vertuous: And there is nothing more proper to depress the Vapours, and to convince her of her Weakness, than to consider all the Movements of her Engine, the Delicateness of her Organs, the (almost) infinite number of Alterations, and painful Failings, to which she is subject.

There is not any Meditation more capable to inspire Humility, Moderation, and Mildness, into a *Man* (whatever he may be), than seriously to mind (by the Study of Natural *Philosophy*) the Union and Tye of his Soul with the Body; and to observe, that he is obnoxious to so many Needs, that the Dependance in which he is (on the most ticklish and delicate Parts of the Body, in his Functions), keeps[75] him constantly exposed to a thousand sorts of Troubles, and irksome Agitations; that, what Knowledge soever he may have entertained, the least thing in the World is enough (entirely) to confound it; that a little Choler, or Blood, more Hot or Cold than ordinary, may cast himself into Extravagance, Folly, and Madness; and make him suffer fearful Convulsions.

When such Reflexions should find Acceptance in the Mind of a *Woman*, as well as of a *Man*, they would chase thence Pride, far from letting of it in. And, if after having filled her Mind with the best of Knowledges, she should call again to her Memory all her by-past Conduct, to see how she had arrived to the happy state, wherein she might find her self very far from elevating of her self above others; she would see enough to humble her the more; since that, she would necessarily observe by that review, that (hereto-fore) she had had an infinite number of Prejudices, which she could not Conquer (but by Strength) against the Impressions of Custom, Example, and Passions; which, in spight of her, engaged her to them: That all the Effects which she had made to discover Truth, had been almost unprofitable: That it hath been, as by Chance, that it hath presented it self to her; and at that time, when she the least dreamt thereof; and in such Occurencies, which happen but once in ones Life, and but to very few Persons: From whence, she would infallibly conclude, That it is unjust, and ridiculous, to slight and despise those who have less Knowledge than our selves, or who embrace contrary Opinions; and that we ought the rather to have Complacency and Compassion for them; because, if they discerne not Truth as we do, it is not their Fault; but, because that it hath not presented it self to them, when they have been in search thereof: and that there is still some Veil on their Part or ours, that hinders it to appear to their mind, in its full Light. And, considering that she might have held for true, that which she had believed false before, she would judge without doubt, That it might still happen in the Sequel, that she might make new Discoveries; by the which, she might believe false or erroneous, that which had appeared to her most true, and certain.

If there have been some *Women*, who (affected with their Knowledge) have become disdainfull; there are likewise a great many Men that dayly fall into the same vice; And that ought not to be considered as an effect of the Sciences, which they have possessed, but because men have looked[76] on them as a Mystery to the Sex: And as, on the one hand, such knowledges are ordinarily very confused; and on the other, they that have them, propose to themselves thereby a particular advantage; it is not to be thought strange that they take occasion from thence to swell, and it is almost unavoidably necessary that in this condition, it should not be with them, as with those who from a low birth, and fortune, have with difficulty raised themselves to honour, and fame: who seeing themselves advanced to a pitch, to which, few of their quality have been accustomed to mount, are seized with a giddiness, which presents to them, objects quite other-wayes than in themselves they are. At least, it is most probable, that seeing the pretended vanity of the learned *Women*, is nothing in comparison of that of the learned men, who arrogate to themselves, the title of Masters and Sages: *Women* would be less Subject thereunto, if their Sex were admitted into equal share with ours, of the advantages which occasion it.

It is then a vulgar Errour to fancy, that Learning is useless to *Women*, because says one, they have no share in Offices, for the which, men apply themselves thereto. It is as necessary to them as Felicity, and Vertue; because without that, we cannot perfectly possess either the one or other. It is so for the purchasing, of Exactness in our thoughts, and Justice in our actions: it is so, for the right Knowledge of our Selves, and what is about us, that we may make the right and lawfull use thereof; and that we may regulate our passions by Moderating of our desires. To become capable of places and dignities, is one of the uses of Learning; and to be fit to be a Judge or Bishop, we should strive to acquire as much as possible, because without it the functions of such Offices cannot be well discharged, but not precisely for that end, and for to become more happy by the possession of the honours, and advantages which they afford: That would be to abuse learning by a sordid and base end.

So that there is nothing but weakness,[77] or a secret and blind interest which can make men say, that *Women* ought to remain shut out from Learning, for this reason, that they have never been publickly admitted to any share therein. It fareth not with the goods of the mind, as with the goods of the body; against them there is no prescription: and how long soever, we have been deprived thereof, we have alwayes the right of Reversion. But it being impossible that the same goods of the body, could at the same time, be possessed by several persons, without domination on each side; men have had reason for the safety of families, to maintain the possessours, with good conscience, in prejudice of the ancient proprietaries.

But, as concerning the advantages of the mind, it goes quite otherwayes. Every one hath a right to all that is intelligible, and good sense. The Spring of reason is not limited; it hath in all men an equal Jurisdiction; we are all born Judges of what touches and affects us; And if we cannot dispose of the same with equal power, we may at least, all know them with a like right. And as all men employ the use of the light and air, without prejudice to any person, by that communication, all may likewise possess the Knowledge of truth without hurting one another. For the more that it is known, the more it appears splendid, and lovely: The greater are the number of those that search after it, and the sooner they find it: And if both Sexes, had equally busied themselves therein, it had still the sooner been discovered. In so much then, that Truth and Knowledge are goods which admit of no prescription; And such that have been deprived thereof, may make a Re-entry, without doing injury to those who are already Masters of the same; There can be none, but such as would rule mens minds by belief, and credit, that have reason to apprehend this Reversion, for fear, that if Sciences should become so common, glory might also; and that the Fame to which they aspire, should be lessened by partnership.

Women are as Capable of Offices[78] and Employments in civil Society as Men are.

There is therefore no inconvenience, if Women apply themselves to Study and Learning as well as we. They are able to make a very good use of them, and to draw from thence the two Advantages which we expect therefrom; the one, to have clear and distinct Knowledges, which we naturally desire, and whereof the desire is often stifled, and annihilated by the confusion of thoughts, and the cares, and agitations of life: And the other, To employ these Knowledges, for the particular conduct of themselves, and for that of others in the different conditions of Society, of which they make a part. This agrees not at all[79] with the Common Opinion. There are indeed many that will believe, that Women may Learn what is to be attained by the Physicks or Natural Sciences; but will not admit, that they are as fit as Men for those which may be called Civil, as Ethicks, Laws, and Politicks; and that if they should be able by the Maximes of these Last, to conduct themselves, they could not therefore be capable of guiding of others.

Men entertain this thought, because, they consider not, that the mind in it's actions, hath need of no more but Discerning, and Exactitude, and whosoever hath once these two qualities in one thing, may as easily, and by the same means have them in all the rest. The being Moral or Civil, changeth not the nature of our actions: They continue to be still Natural: Because that Morality is nothing else, but to know the manner, how men regard the actions of others, with Relation to the Notions which they have of good or evil, of vice and vertue, of justice and injustice; And as that, when we have once rightly conceived the Rules of Motion, in Natural *Philosophy*, we may apply them to all the changes, and varieties which are remarked in Nature: So likewise knowing once the true principles of civil Sciences, there remains no more difficulty to make application thereof to the new, and incident Emergents which occurr.

They that are in places have not alwayes more wit, though they have better Luck than others: And indeed it is not necessary, that they should have more, than the common; though it were[80] to be wished, that none were admitted to employments but the most worthy. We act still after the same manner, and by the same Rules, in what estate soever, we find our selves; unless it be that the more our conditions are raised, the more our cares and views are extended, because we have the more to do. And all the change which happens to men who are placed above others, is like to that of a person who being mounted to the top of a Tower, carryes his prospect farther, and discovers more different objects, than they who stay on the ground below: It is their favors, if *Women* be as capable as we are to guid themselves, they are likewise to conduct others, and to have place in charges and dignities of Civil Society.

The most Simple, and natural use that we can make of Sciences which we have well learned, is to teach them to others: And if *Women* had studied in the Universities with men, or in others appointed for them in particular, they might have entred into Degrees, and taken the title of Master of Arts, Doctor of Divinity, Medicine, Civil, and Cannon Law: And their genius so advantagiously fitting them to learn, would dispose them likewise to teach with success. They would find methods, and insinuating biasses, to instill their Doctrine; they would discover the strength and weakness of their Schollars, to proportion themselves to their reach, and the facility which they have to express themselves; and, which is one of the most excellent talents of a good Master, would compleat and render them admirable Mistresses.

The employment which approacheth most to a School-Master, is that of Pastour or Minister in the Church, and there can be nothing else but custome shewn, which remove *Women* there-from. They have a Spirit as well as we, capable of the Knowledge and love of God, and thereby able to incline others to know, and love him. Faith is common to them with us: And the Gospel with the Promises thereof, are likewise addressed to them. Charity also comprehends them in its duties; and, if they know how to put in practice the actions thereof, may not they likewise publickly teach its Maxims? Whosoever can preach by Example, from stronger reason can do so by Words: And a *Woman* that should join her Natural Eloquence with the Morality of *Jesus Christ*, should be as capable as another, to Exhort, Direct,[81] Correct, admit into Christian Society those who deserved. And cut off such who after having submitted themselves thereto, should refuse to observe the Rules thereof. And if men were accustomed to see *Women* in a Pulpit, they would be no more startled thereat, than the *Women*[82] are at the sight of men.

We are not assembled into Society, but that we may live in peace, and find, in a Mutual assistance, all that is necessary for the Body, and Soul.[83] This we could not enjoy without trouble, if there were no authority; that is to say, that for that end, there ought to be some persons who have power to make Laws, and to inflict punishment upon the breakers of them. And to make the right use of that authority, we must know to what it obligeth and be perswaded that those who possess it, ought to have no other design in the discharge thereof, but to procure the welfare and advantage of their inferiours. *Women* being no less susceptible of this perswasion than men, may not we then submit our selves to them, and consent not only not to resist their Orders, but even contribute as much as we can to oblige to obedience such as make any difficulty therein?

So that nothing needed to hinder, but that a *Woman* might sit upon a Throne, and that for the government of her people, She might study their humour, the interests, their Lawes, their customes, and their practices: That she might place in Offices[84] of the Gown and Sword, only able and deserving persons; and, in the Dignities of the Church, men of understanding and Example. Is it a thing so difficult, that a *Woman* could not perform it, to instruct her-self of the strength, and weakness of a State, and of those that lay round it; to entertain amongst strangers secret Intelligences for to discover their designes, and disappoint their measures, and to have faithfull Spies, and Emissaries in all Suspected places; to be exactly informed of all that passeth there, wherein she might have interest? Is there needfull for the conduct of a Kingdome more vigilance, and application than *Women* have for their families, or the Religious for their Convents? They would prove no less refined in publick Negotiations, than they are in private affairs. And as piety and mildness is natural to their Sex, their government would prove less Rigorous than that of many Princes, and we should wish for under their Reign, that which is often feared under that of many others, that Subjects would regulate themselves according to the Example of their Governours.

We may easily conclude, that if *Women* are capable to possesse severally all publick authority, they are still more to be subordinate Officers and Ministers: As Vice-Queens, Governants, Secretaries, Counsellors of State, and Treasurers.

For my part, I should be no more surprized to see a *Woman* with a helmet on her head, than to see her with a Crown; preside in a Council of warr, as well as in a Council of State: To see her train, and exercise her Souldiers, drawing them up in Battel-array, and divide them in several Bodyes, and Squadrons, with as much ease as she would please her self to see it done. The military Art hath nothing beyond others, whereof *Women* are not capable, unless it be that it is somewhat more rude, causeth greater noise, and does more mischief. The Eyes are sufficient to learn from a Mapp, that is somewhat exact, all the High-wayes of a countrey, the good and bad[85] passages, and the places that are most proper for suprizes, and encampings. There is hardly a Souldier that is not ready to know that a General ought first to gain all the Passes before he venture there his forces, regulate all his enterprizes according to the advice of good Scouts; And even deceive the Army by Wiles, and counter-marches the better to cover his design. A *Woman* can do all this, and can invent Stratagems to surprise the enemy, put the wind and dust in his teeth, and the Sun in his face:[86] And Charging him on one side, Flank him on the other; Give him false allarms, draw him into an ambush by a feigned flight; give battel, and be the first that mounts a breach to encourage the Souldiers; Perswasion, and passion does all: And *Women* testifie no less heat, and resolution when their honour is concerned, than is requisite to attack or defend a Place.

What can be reasonably objected, why a *Woman* of sound Judgement and Understanding, might not take the chaire in a court of Justice,[87] and preside in all other companies. There are a great many able men who would learn the Lawes and Customes of a state with less trouble, than some Games at Cards, which *Women* understand so well: And it is as easy to remember them, as an intire Romance; is it not as easy to see into the heart of an affair, as to trace an intrigue upon the Stage, and make as faithfull report of a Law suite, as of a Comedy? All these things are alike easy, to those who equally apply themselves thereto.

Now seeing there is neither office, nor imployment in society which is not comprehended in these whereof we have spoken, nor where there is greater need of knowledge or parts: it must be confest, that *Women* are proper for all.

Besides, the Natural dispositions of the body, and the Notions which men have of the function and duties of their places, there is still somewhat necessary that renders them more or less capable to acquit themselves worthy thereof. The true perswasion of what a man is obliged to do, the consideration of Religion, and interest, emulation betwixt equals, desire of winning glory, and Honour, and of making, preserving, or increasing ones fortitude.[88] According as a man is more or less touched with these things, his management is altogether different: And *Women* being no less sensible thereof than men, in regard of employments, they want nothing to render them their equals.[89]

We may (then) with Assurance exhort Ladies to apply themselves to Study; without having Respect to the little Reasons of those who would undertake to divert them there from. Since they have a Mind (as well as we) capable of knowing of Truth (which is the only Subject, on which they can employ their Pains worthily), they ought to put themselves in condition of avoyding the Reproach, of having stifled a Talent, which they might put to use; and of having detained Truth in Idleness and Pleasure. There is no other way for them to Guard themselves against Errour, and the Surprize to which they are exposed (who Learn nothing but by the manner of *Gazets*; that is to say, upon the bare word of another), nor to render themselves happy in this Life, by practicing Vertue with Discretion.

What Advantage soever they propose to themselves besides this, they would meet with it in Study. If their Parlours were turned into Academies, their Entertainments would be Greater, more Solid, and more Pleasing. And every one may judge, of the Satisfaction she should have to Discourse of Lofty Matters, by the Content that she hath to hear others speak thereof. How slight soever might be the Subjects of their Conversation, they would have the Pleasure to treat them more wittily than the Vulgar: And the delicate Manners, which are so peculiar to their Sex (being fortified by solid Reasons and Arguments) would far more sensibly affect the Hearers.

They who only desire to please, would there (to Admiration) find their Designe; For, the Splendour of the Beauty of Body, being heightened by that of the Mind, would thereby become a hundred times more Brisk and Lively. And, as *Women* (but of ordinary Beauty) are alwayes well regarded when they are Witty,[90] the Advantages of the Mind, Cultivated by Study, would give them Means abundantly to supply what Nature or Fortune might have denied them. They would be admitted into the Entertainments of the Learned, and reigne amongst them upon a double Respect: They would enter into the Management of Affairs: Their Husbands would not refuse to abandon to them the Conduct of their Families, and to take their Advice in all things. And, seeing that Matters are in such a state, that they cannot (now) be admitted into Charges, (at least) they might be able to know the Nature of Functions, and judge if they be deservingly bestowed.

The Difficulty of arriving to this Pitch, ought not to scare them: It is not so great as *Men* have made it. That which is the cause, why *Men* think there is need of so much Trouble, for to gain a few Knowledges, is, Because they teach (for that end) a great many things, which are most unprofitable for those that aspire thereto. All Knowledge (even to this present) consisting only in possessing of a *History* of the Sentiments of those that are gone before us; and *Men*, having too much reposed on Custom, and the Credit[91] of their Masters, very few have the good Luck to find the Natural Method. Herein we might labour, and make appear, That *Men* render themselves qualified in far less time, and with a great deal more Pleasure, than is ordinarily imagined.

That Women *have an Advantagious Disposition for Sciences; and that the true Notions of Perfection, Nobility, and Honesty, suit with them as well as* Men.

Hitherto, we have considered nothing in *Women*, but the Head; and, it hath appeared, that that Part (taken in general) hath in them as much Proportion for all Sciences (whereof it is the Organ), as in *Men*. Nevertheless, because that this Organ is not altogether alike, even amongst all *Men* themselves; and that there are a great many, in whom it is more proper for some things than for others: we must descend a little lower into the Particular, to see if there be nothing in *Women*, that renders them less fit for Learning, than our selves.

We may observe, that they have a Countenance more stately and happy than we: They have the Forehead high, lofty, and large; which is the usual mark of Witty and Imaginative[92] Persons. And, we find in effect, that *Women* have much Vivacity, Fancy, and Memory; which denotes a Brain so disposed, that it easily receives the Impressions of Objects, even of the most Slight and Inconsiderable, which escape such, as are of another Disposition; and that it retains them without trouble, and presents them to the Mind in the instant that it stands in need thereof.

When this Disposition is accompanied with Heat, it renders the Mind more ready and quick to be affected by the Objects; to fasten on, and penetrate, into them the more; and to extend the Images, and Impressions thereof, at pleasure: From whence, it happens, that they who have good Imaginations (considering things on more sides, and in less time), are very Ingenious, and Inventive; and discover more with one only Glance, than many others after much Attention. They are fit to represent things with an insinuating and pleasing strain, and to find, on the Spot, Turns and proper Expedients: They express themselves with Facility and Grace; and set off their Thoughts with the Greatest Advantage.[93]

All this is Remarkable in *Women*; and, I can see nothing in this Disposition, which is inconsistent with a good Wit. Judgement, and Exactness, make the Natural Character thereof; to acquire which two good Qualities, we must become a little Sedentary, and dwell on Objects; to the end, that we may avoid the Errour and Mistake, wherein *Men* fall by skipping. It is true, that the multitude of Thoughts, in brisk Persons, hurries (many times) the Imagination; But, it is likewise true, That, by Exercise, it may be fixed. We have the Experience of this, in the greatest *Men* of this Age; who, for the most part, are all very imaginative.

It may be affirmed, That this Temper is the fittest for Society; and that *Men*, not being made to remain alwayes alone, and shut up in a Closet; we ought (in some measure) the more to esteem those who have the best Disposition, pleasingly and profitably to Communicate their Thoughts.

And *Women*, who have naturally Wit, (because they have Fancy, Memory, and a sparkling Liveliness,) may with a little Application, acquire the Qualities of a good Judgement.

This is sufficient to prove, That, in Respect of the Head alone, the *Two Sexes* are Equal. There are Observations upon the rest of the Body, which are most Curious; but of which, we must only speak in passing.

Men have alwayes had this common ill Luck, to spill and shed[94] (if we may so say) their Passions on all the Works of Nature: There is not any Notion, which they have not blended with some touch of Love or Hatred, of Esteem or Contempt: And these which concern the Distinction of the *Two Sexes*, are so material, and so befogg'd[95] with the Sentiments of Imperfection, Baseness, Undecency, and other Trifles; that, seeing they cannot be touched without moving of some Passion, and stirring up the Flesh against the Spirit, it is often Prudence to let them alone.

And yet, it is upon that odd Medley, of alwayes confused Notions, that the Opinions disadvantagious to *Women*, are founded; and which the small Wits (ridiculously) use to mortifie them. The justest Mean and Temper, that can be betwixt the necessity of explaining ones Self, and the Difficulty of doing it Innocently, is, To observe what we ought (Rationally) to understand by Perfection and Imperfection, by Nobility and Baseness, and by Decency and Undecency.

When I conceive that there is a *God*, I easily conceive, that all things depend on Him: And if, after having considered the Natural and Intrinsical State of Creatures, which consists (if they be Bodies) in the Disposition of their Parts, with a Reference to one another; and the Extrinsical, which is the Relation that they stand in, to act or suffer with other Beings that environ them: If (I say) I enquire into the Reason of these two Conditions, I can find, none other but the Will and Pleasure of Him who is the Author of them. I observe further, that Bodies have (ordinarily) a certain Disposition, which renders them capable to produce and receive certain Effects; For example, that *Man* can understand by the help of his Ears, the Thoughts of others, and by the Instruments of Voice, express to them his own. And I Remark, that Bodies are uncapable of such Effects, when they are otherwise disposed: From whence, I inform my self of two Notions; whereof, the one Represents to me, the First State of Things, with all their necessary Consequences; and that I call the State of *Perfection*; And the other, the Condition contrary; which I name *Imperfection*.

So, a *Man* (in my Esteem) is Perfect, when he hath all that he needeth (according to Divine Institution), for the producing and receiving the Effects to which he is appointed: And, he is imperfect, when he hath more or fewer Parts, than are necessary; or any Indisposition that removes him from this end.

Wherefore, he being formed in such manner, that he hath need of Aliment for Subsistence, I look not upon that Necessity, as an Imperfection; no more, than the Need which is coupled with the use of Food; that, what is Superfluous, must be avoided out of the Body. I find also, that all Creatures are equally Perfect, as long as they continue in their natural and ordinary State.

We must not confound Perfection with Nobility: These are two things very different. Two Creatures may be Equal in Perfection, and in Nobility Unequal.

When I make Reflexion upon my Self, it seems to me, that my Spirit (being only capable of Knowledge) ought to be preferred to my Body, and be considered as the most Noble: And, when I consider Bodies, without any Respect to my Self; that is to say, without reflecting, that they may be profitable or hurtful to me, pleasing or displeasing; I cannot perswade my self, that one is more Noble than another, being all but made of matter diversely Figured. Yet, when I medle with Bodies (considering the Good or Hurt that they do to me), I come to esteem them differently. Although that my Head (regarded without Interest) affects me no more, than the other Parts; nevertheless, I prefer it to all the rest, when I come to think, that it is of greater importance to me, in the Union of the Spirit with the Body.

For the same Reason it is, that, although all the Places of the Body be equally perfect, we have (nevertheless) different Esteems for them: The very Parts themselves (whereof the Use is most necessary) being many times considered with some sort of Contempt and Aversion; because that the Use is less pleasing, or otherwise. It is so with all that surround and affects us; For, that which makes that one thing pleaseth one *Man*, and displeaseth another, is, that it hath made impression upon them differently.

It is the Engagement of *Men* in Society, that produceth in them the Notion of Decency: So that, although it be neither Imperfection nor Baseness, to ease and comfort the Body; and that it is even a Necessity, and Indispensable Consequence of its Natural Disposition; and that all the wayes of doing thereof, are Equal; there are some notwithstanding, that are considered less Decent; because they are more offensive to the Persons, in whose Presence they are performed.

As all Creatures, and all their Actions, being considered in themselves, and without any reference to Custom or Esteem that is made thereof, are as Perfect, and as Noble, the one as the other; they are likewise equally Decent, being considered in the same manner. Wherefore, we may say, that the Regards of Decency and Undecency are almost all, in their Original, nothing else but the Effects of Imagination, and the Capriciousness of *Men*. This appears by that, That one thing which is Decent in one Countrey, is not all so in another; and that, in the same Kingdome, but in divers places,[96] or (in the same time) but among Persons of different Condition, Quality, and Humour; the same Action is sometime conforme, sometime contrary to Decency. So that, Decency is nothing but the manner of using of Natural Things, according to the Esteem which *Men* pass upon them; and to which, it is Prudence to Conform.

We are all possessed with this Notion; although we make no Reflexion thereon, that all Persons (whether they be our Beloved, or the Witty and Judicious; who in Publick, and according to the ordinary Custom, subject themselves to the Rites of Decency) discharge themselves thereof in Private, as of Burdens troublesome and foolish.

The Case is the same with Nobility. In some Countries of the *Indies*, the Labourers have the same Rank, as the Nobles with us: In some Countries, Sword-Men are preferred to the Gown-Men; And in others, the quite contrary is Practised: Every one, according as his Inclinations leads him to favour such States, or that he esteems them most Important.

Comparing these Notions, with the Opinions that the Vulgar have of *Women*; we shall (without trouble) discover wherein consisteth the Errour.

From whence is derived, the Distinction of Sexes; How far it extends it self: And that it places no Difference betwixt Men and Women, with Relation to Vice and Vertue: And that the Temperament, and Constitution in general, in it self, is neither good nor bad.

God willing to produce *Men* in Dependence, one upon another, by the Concourse of two Persons; for that end, framed two Bodies, which were different: Each was perfect in its kind; and they might ought both to be disposed, as they are at present: And all that depends on their particular Constitution, ought to be considered, as making a part of their Perfection.

It is then without Reason, that some imagine, That *Women* are not so perfect as *Men*; and that they look upon that (in them) as a Defect, which is an Essential Portion of their Sex; without the which, it would be useless for the end, for which it hath been formed; which begins and ceases with Fecundity, and which is destin'd for the most excellent use of the World; that is, to frame and nourish us in their Bellies.[97]

The *Two Sexes* (together) are necessary to beget the like: And if we knew, how it is that ours contribute thereto, we should find enough to be said against ourselves. It is hard to be understood, upon what they ground themselves, who maintain, That *Men* are more Noble than *Women*, in regard of Children; since it is properly the *Women* who Conceive us,

Form us, and give us Life, Birth, and Breeding. It is true, they pay dearer for it than we: But their Pain and Trouble ought not to be Prejudicial to *them*, and draw upon *them* Contempt, in place of Esteem, which they thereby deserve.

Who would say, That Fathers and Mothers (who labour to bring up their Children, good Princes to Govern their Subjects, and Magistrates to render them Justice,) are less Estimable than they whose Aid and Assistance they use, for to discharge themselves of their Duties?

There are some *Physitians*, who have mightily enlarged themselves upon the Temperament of *Sexes*, to the Disadvantage of *Women*; and have pursued their Discourses out of sight; to shew, That their *Sex* ought to have a Constitution altogether different from ours, which renders it inferiour in all things. But their Reasons are only light Conjectures; which come into the Heads of such, as judge of things only by Prejudice, and upon simple Appearances.

When they perceive the *Two Sexes* more distinguished, by that which regards the civil, than particular, Functions; they fancy to themselves, that so they ought to be; And, not discerning exactly enough, betwixt that which proceeds from Custom and Education, and that which comes from Nature; they have attributed to one and the same Cause, all which they see in Society; imagining, that when *God* Created *Man* and *Woman*, he disposed them in such a manner, as ought to produce all the Distinction which we observe betwixt them.

This is to carry too far the Difference of *Sexes*: It ought to be bounded by the Designe, which *God* hath had to form *Men*, by the Concourse of two Persons; and no more to be admitted, but what is necessary for that Effect.

We see, that *Men* and *Women* are alike (almost) in all, as to the inward and outward Constitution of the Body; and that the Natural Functions (on which depends our Conservation) are performed in both, after the same manner. It is then enough to the end, that they may give Birth to a Third; that there be some Organs in the one, which are not in the other: And yet, it is not necessary in respect of that, (as *Men* imagine) that *Women* have less Strength and Vigour than Men.

And, as there is nothing but Experience, that can enable us to judge aright of that Distinction; do not we find, that *Women* are mixed, as we are? There are some both Strong and Weak in both *Sexes*. *Men* brought up in Softness and Ease, are worse than *Women*; and sink at first under Labour: But when (by Necessity, or otherwise) they are hardened, they become Equal, and sometimes Superiour to others.

It is just so with *Women*: They that are taken up and employed in painful Exercises, are stronger than *Ladies*, who only handle the Needle. And this may encline us to think, that if both *Sexes* were equally Exercised, the one might acquire as much Vigour as the other; which, in former times, have been seen in a Common-Wealth;[98] where Wrestling, and other Exercises, were common to *both*: The same is Reported of the *Amazones*, in the South Part of *America*.

We ought not (then) to lay any ground on certain ordinary Expressions, drawn from the present State of the *Two Sexes*. When we would (mockingly) blame a *Man*, as having little Courage, Resolution, and Constancy, we call him *Effeminate*; as if we would say, That he is as Low, and Cowhearted, as a *Woman*. On the other hand, to praise a *Woman* that is above the Ordinary, because of her Courage, Strength, or Wit; we say, She is a *Man*. These Expressions (so advantagious to *Men*) do not a little Contribute, to entertain the high Notion that we have of *them*; Because we consider not, that they are but Likely-hoods; and that their Verity indifferently supposes Nature, or Custom; and so, are purely Contingent, and Arbitrary. Vertue, Mildness, and Integrity, being so peculiar to *Women* (if their Sex had not been so little esteemed); when we would have signified, with Elogy, that a *Man* had all these Qualities in an Eminent Degree; we would have said, He is a *Woman*, if it had so pleased *Men*, to Establish this form of Speech.

What-ever the Matter be, it is not the Strength of the Body, that ought to distinguish *Man-kind*; otherwise, Beasts would have the advantage of *them*; and, amongst our Selves, the Strongest. Notwithstanding, we know by Experience, that such who have so great Strength, are proper for nothing but

Material[99] Works: And that these, on the other hand, who have less, have commonly more Brains. The ablest *Philosophers*, and the greatest Princes, have been Delicate enough; and the greatest Generals, would not have (perhaps) been willing to Wrestle with the meanest of their Souldiers. Go but to a Court of Justice, and you shall see, whether the greatest Judge match alwayes (in Strength) the lowest of their Officers.

It is then useless, to lean so much upon the Constitution of the Body, for to render Reason of the Difference which is seen betwixt the *Two Sexes*, in Relation to the Spirit.

The Temperament does not consist in an indivisible Point: For, as we cannot find two Persons in whom it is altogether alike; neither can we any more determine, precisely, wherein it is that they differ. There are many sorts of *Cholericks, Sanguines*, and *Melancholicks*; and all these Diversities hinder not, but that they may be often as capable the one, as the other; and that there may be excellent *Men*, of all sorts of Constitutions: And even supposing, that that of the *Two Sexes* be as different, as it is pretended to be; there is still found greater Difference amongst many *Men*, who are (notwithstanding) believed capable of the same things. The More, and the Less, being so little considerable, there is nothing, but a spirit of Wrangling, that can make it be regarded.

It is probable, that that which engrosseth so much (into Notion) the Distinction whereof we speak, is, That *Men* examine not precisely enough, all that which is Remarkable in *Women*: And that Defect makes us fall into the Errour of those, who (having the Mind confused) distinguish not aright, what (severally) belongs to things; and attribute to one, that which only pertains to another; because they find them together in the same Subject. Wherefore, finding so great Difference in *Women*, as to the manner of Actions, and Functions; *Men* have transferred it to the Temperament, for want of Knowledge of the true Cause.

However it be, if we would examine, which is the most Excellent of the *Two Sexes*, by the comparing of Bodies; *Women* might pretend to the Advantage, and without insisting on the Internal Fabrick of their Bodies; and that it is in them, that the thing in the World (the most Curious to be known) passeth; to wit, How that *Man* (the most Beautiful and Wonderful of all Creatures) is produced: Who can hinder them to say, That that which appeareth in the outside, ought to give them the better? That Comeliness, and Beauty, are natural and peculiar to them; and that it is this, that produceth Effects as sensible, as ordinary: And that, if what they can performe by the inside of the Head, renders them (at least) *Mens* Equals; the Out-side seldome ever failes, to render them absolutely their Mistresses.

Beauty being as real an Advantage, as Strength and Health, Reason forbiddeth not to plead Pre-eminence therefrom, rather than from the others: and if we should judge of its Value (by the Sentiments and Passions, which it excites), as we judge (for the most part) of all things; we would find, that there is nothing more estimable, there being nothing so effective; that is to say, which moves and stirs more Passions, and does mingle and fortifie them more diversly, as the Impressions of Beauty.

It would not at all be necessary, to speak any more concerning the Temperament of *Women;* if an Author (no less Famous than Polite) had not thought fit to consider it, as the force of the Defects which *Men* commonly charge them with; which helps much to confirm People in the Opinion, That they are less to be valued than we. Without relating his Opinion, I say, that for the right examining of the Temperament of the *Two Sexes* (with a Reference to Vice and Vertue), it must be considered in a State indifferent; when, as yet, neither Vice nor Vertue were in Nature: And then we shall find, that that which in one time is called Vertue, may in another, pass for Vice (according to the use that *Men* make thereof); So that, in that case, all Temperaments are alike.

For the better Understanding of this Opinion, we must observe, that there is nothing but our Soul capable of Vertue; which, in general, consists in a firm and constant Resolution, of doing that which we judge, the best; according to the divers Occurencies that we meet with. The Body (properly) is nothing but the Organ, and Instrument of that Resolution (as a Sword in ones hand), both for Offence and Defence: And all the different Dispositions (which renders it more or less fit for that use), ought not to be called good or bad; but as their Effects are more ordinary, and important, for Good and Evil: For example, The Disposition to Flight, for avoyding the Evils which threaten us, is Indifferent; because there are some, which cannot otherwise be shunned; and then, it is Wisdom to flye: When, on the other hand, it is culpable Cowardice, for one to betake himself to his Heels, when the Danger is superable, by a generous Resistance; which produceth more Good than Hurt.

But the Mind is no less capable in *Women,* than in *Men,* of that firm Resolution, which makes up Vertue; not of knowing the Ran-counters, when it is to be put in Practice. They can Regulate their Passions, as well as we; and are not more enclined to Vice, than to Vertue. We might even make the Ballance turn to their Favour on this side; since that the Affection towards Children (without comparison, stronger in *Women,* than in *Men*), is naturally linked to Compassion; which we may call, the Vertue and Bond of Civil Society: It being impossible to conceive, That Society is rationally Established for other end, than to supply the common Wants and Necessities of one another. And if we nearly observe, How Passions are formed in us; we shall find, that after the manner that *Women* contribute to the Production and Education of *Men,* it is as a Natural Consequence; that they should treat them in the Afflictions, in some sort as their Children.

The Difference which is observed, between Men and Women, in regard of Manners, proceeds from the Education which is given Them.

It is so much the more important to Remark, That the Dispositions, which we bring with us into the World, are neither (in their Nature)[100] good or bad; that otherwise, we cannot avoyd an Errour very ordinary; whereby *Men* often refer to Nature, that which (onely) springs from Custom.

Men torture their Minds, to search for a Reason, Why we are subject to certain Faults, and have particular Customs; for want of having observed, that which may be produced in us, by Habit, Exercise, *Education,* and outward Condition; that is to say, The Relation of Sex, Age, Fortune, and Employment, wherein we are placed in Society: It being certain, that all these different Views diversifying, in an infinite number of wayes, the thoughts, and passions, answerably dispose the minds quite other-wayes, to look on the truths presented to them. It is for that Reason, that the same Maxime, proposed at the same time to Citizens, Souldiers, to Judges, and Princes, affects them, and makes them Act so differently: Because, that *Men* caring for nothing but the out-side; Look on it as the Rule, and measure of their Sentiments: Whence happens, that the one lets pass as useless, that which very much takes up others; That Sword-men are Choaked with that which flatters Gown-men: And that Persons of the same Constitution take sometimes certain things in a contrary Sense; Which enter by one and the same bias into the minds of Persons of different temperament; but who have same the fortune, or education.

It is not that we pretend, that all men bring into the World the same bodily constitution. That would be indeed, an ill-grounded pretence. There are some that are quick, and some slow: but it appeareth not, that that diversity any way hinders the minds to receive the same instruction: all that, it does, is, that some receive it more readily and happily than others. So that what temperament soever *Women* have, they are no less capable than we, of truth and studies. And if we find at present, in some of them some defect, or impediment; or even that all of them, do not look into solid matters, as men do; to which notwithstanding experience is contrary, that ought solely to be rejected upon the outward condition of their Sex, and on the education, which is given them, which comprehends the ignorance wherein they are left, the Prejudices or Errours, which are instilled in them, the Example which they have of others their like. And all the wayes to which *Decorum*, restraint, reserve, subjection, and fears, reduceth them.

In effect, nothing is omitted, on their account which may serve to perswade them, that this great difference, which they see betwixt their Sex, and ours, is a work of Reason, or divine institution. The apparel, education, and exercise, cannot be more different. A Maid is not in security but under the wings of her Mother; or under the eyes of a Governant that never leaves her: They Frighten her with every thing: Threaten her with Spirits, and Hobgoblines, in all the corners of the house, where she may be alone: Even in the streets, and Churches, there is something to be feared, if she have not her guards. The great care which is taken to dress her; takes up all her mind: So many lookes as are glanced at her, and so many discourses, which she heares of beauty, imploves all her thoughts; And the complements, which she receives on this Subject, make[101] her therein place all her happiness. As they never speak to her of any thing else, with that she limits all her designs, and carryes no higher her prospects. Dancing, writing, and reading, are the greatest exercises of *Women;* all their library consists in a few little Bookes of Devotion; with that which is in the little cabinet.

All their Science is reduced to work with a Needle. The Looking Glass is the great Master and Oracle which they consult. Balls, Playes, and the Modes, make the subject of their Entertainments: They consider their meetings as, famous Accademies, whither[102] they go to inform themselves of all the news of their Sex. And if it happen, that some one or other distinguish themselves from the common, by the reading of certain Bookes, which they had trouble enough to catch, thereby to unlock their minds, they are often obliged to hide themselves: The greatest part of their companions, out of Jealousie or other respects, never failing to accuse them of intending to play the rare things.[103]

As to Maids of meaner condition, forced to gain their lively-hood by their labour; their parts are still more useless. Care is taken to make them learn a trade convenient to their

Sex, as soon as they are fit thereto, and their necessity of imploying themselves continually therein, hinders them from thinking of any thing else: And when both one, and others of them, bred in this manner have attained to the age of marriage, they are engaged therein, or otherwayes confin'd to a Cloyster, where they go on to live as they have begun.

In all that which is taught to *Women,* do we see any thing that tends to solid instruction? It seems on the contrary, that men have agreed on this sort of education, on[104] purpose to abase their courage, darken their mind, and to fill it only with vanity, and fopperies; there to stifle all the seeds of Vertue, and Knowledge, to render useless all the dispositions which they might have to great things, and to take from them the desire of perfecting themselves, as well as we by depriving them of the means.

When I seriously think on the manner, how men look upon that which they think to see faulty, in *Women,* I find that such a carriage[105] hath in it somewhat beneath persons endowed with reason. If there be equal occasion of finding of fault in both Sexes, that which accuseth the other, offends against Natural equity; if there be more evill in ours, and that we see it not, we are rash to speak of the faults of others; if we see it, and conceal it, we are unjust to blame the other who hath less. If there be more good in *Women,* than in *Men; Men* ought to be accused of ignorance, or envy, not to acknowledge it. When[106] in a *Woman* there is more Vertue than Vice, the one should serve to excuse the other; and when the defects that she hath are insurpassable, or that the means to rid her self thereof, or guard therefrom, are wanting, as to *Woman* they are, such a one deserves compassion, not contempt. In fine, if these defects be but slight, or onely apparent, it is imprudence or Malice to insist on them; And it is not hard to prove, that men commonly carry so in respect of *Women.*

It is commonly said, that they are timerous, and uncapable of defence; that they are afraid of their shadow, that the cry of[107] a child allarmes them, and the whistling of the Wind makes them tremble. That is not Universal. There are a great many *Women* as bold as men, and it is known that the most fearfull make often of necessity a Vertue; timerousness, is almost inseparable from vertue, and all vertuous persons have it: As they would not do hurt to any, and that they are not ignorant how much wickedness is amongst men; a small matter is enough to fill them with fear. It is a Natural passion, from which no body is exempt: all men fear death, and the troubles of life; the most powerfull Princes apprehend the Rebellion of their Subjects, and the invasion of enemies, and the most valiant Generals to be surprized unawares.

Fear is great, proportionably, to the force which men think they have to resist; and it is not blameable, but in such who[108] are strong enough to repell the evill which threatens them: And we should be as unreasonable to accuse a Judge, or a man that had never minded any thing but his Book, of baseness, for refusing to fight a duel; as to blame a Souldier who had alwayes carryed arms, for not daring to enter into dispute against a learned *Philosopher.*

Women are bred in a manner that gives them ground to apprehend, and fear every thing; they have not light enough to avoid surprizes in matters of Understanding. They have no share in the exercises which give strength and dexterity for attacking, and defending; They see themselves exposed helplessly to suffer the outragiousness of a Sex so[109] subject to Transports,[110] which regards them with contempt, and that often treats its like with more rage, and cruelty, than Wolves do one another.

Wherefore timerousness in *Women* ought not to pass for a defect, but rather for a Rational passion, to which they owe modesty, which is so peculiar to them; and the two great advantages of life, which are the inclination to Vertue; and the aversion from Vice, which the greatest part of men with all the education and light which are given them, can hardly acquire.

Fear of want is the ordinary cause of Avarice, *Men* are no less subject thereunto than *Women;* And if we came to an account, I know not if the number of the first should not be found greater, and their covetousness more blame worthy;

Since the middle[111] Vertue is not far distant from the two Vices, the Extreams, men often mistake the one for the other, and confound avarice with laudable frugality.

As the same action may be good in one, and bad in[112] another, it often happens that that which is evill in us, is not at all so in *Women:* They are destitute of all means to make their fortunes by their parts,[113] the door of Sciences, and Employments, being shut against them; And so being in worse condition to guard themselves against the misfortunes, and inconvenieces of life, they ought more to be concerned. It is no wonder then, that herewith they seeing what a great trouble it is to purchase a small estate, they take care to keep it.

If they receive so easily that which is told them, it is an effect of their candour, and ingenuity, that will not suffer them to think, that these who have authority over them, are ignorant, or interested; and we offend Justice, to accuse them of credulity, since there is yet more amongst us. The ablest men suffer themselves to be too much allured by a false appearance; And all their Knowledge is often times, but a mean credulity, but of somewhat greater extent than that of *Women:* I mean, that they are not more knowing than others; but because they have more Lightly given their consent, to a greater number of things, of which they have retained the Notions, right or wrong, by having so often run them over.

That which causeth timerousness in *Women,* produceth likewise superstition, which the learned themselves impute to them: But in this, the learned appear like those, who being most in the wrong, perswade themselves that they are in the right, because they make a Lowder Noise than others. They fancy that they themselves, are clear from superstition, because they find it in some ignorant *Women,* whil'st in the mean time, themselves are therein miserably plunged up to the eares.

Though all men were the true worshipers of God, in Spirit, and in Truth, and that *Women* rendered him only Superstitious adoration, in this they would be excusable. They are not at all taught to know God by themselves: they know nothing of him, but what is told them: And, as the most part of *Men* speak of him in a manner, so unworthy of what he is, and distinguish him not from his Creatures, but only by the attribute of Creator; it is no wonder, that *Women* only knowing upon their report, Worship him by Religion, with the same Sentiments that they have for men, whom they fear and reverence.

There are some men, that think they can sufficiently Mortifie the *Women,* by telling of them, that they are nothing else all of them but tatlers. They have reason to be vexed, at so impertinent a calumny. Their body is so happily disposed by the temperament which is proper[114] to them, that they distinctly retain the impressions of Objects, which once they have received: They represent them to themselves without Trouble, and express them with wonderful Facility: That is the Reason, that the Notions which they have, awakening on the least occasion, they begin and continue their Conversation at their Pleasure: And the Quickness of their Spirit (giving them Means to perceive, easily, the Relations of things among themselves, they)[115] pass without trouble from one Subject to another; and, by that means, can speak a long time, without letting the Discourse flag or dye.

The Benefit of Speech, is naturally accompanied with a great desire of using it, which occasion offers: It is the only Bond of *Men* in Society; and many find, that there is no greater Pleasure in the World, nor becoming the Mind, than to Communicate their Thoughts to others. Wherefore, *Women* being able to speak with Ease, and being bred and brought up with others; they were to be blamed, if they failed to entertain themselves.

They ought not, then, to pass for Tatlers, but when they speak out of purpose; and of things, which they understand not, without desire of Instruction.

We must not imagine, that People never tatle, but when they talk of Cloths and Fashions. The Tatle of News-Mongers,[116] is often more ridiculous: And that, store of Words, heaped one upon another (and which signifie nothing at all, in the most part of Works), make a Chat far more simple, than that of the silliest of *Women.* At least, we may say, That the Discourses of these, are real and intelligible; and that, they are not vain enough, to imagine (as the greatest part of the Learned do), That they are Wiser than their Neighbours; because they utter more Words, and less Sense. If *Men* had a Tongue as free, it would be impossible to make them hold their Peace. Every one entertains himself with what he knows; Merchants about their Business, *Philosophers* with their Studies, and *Women* about that which they have been able to Learn; And they may say, That they would have entertained themselves better, and with greater Solidity, if there had been as great Care for Instruction taken with *them.*

It choaks a great many, that *Women,* in their Conversation, testifie a great desire to know every thing. I know not what can be the Palat of these *Men,* that cannot relish, that *Women* should be so Curious: For my part, I am well pleased, that People should be curious; and I only advise them, to manage it so, that they be not troublesome therewith.

I look upon the Conversations of *Women,* as upon those of *Philosophers;* where it is equally permitted to all, to entertain themselves about things, of which they have no Knowledge; and there are cross Times in the one, as well as the other.

It is ordinary with many *Men,* to treat the Curious, like Beggars. When they are in an Humour of bestowing, they take it not ill to be asked; and when they have a mind to discover what they know, they are glad to be entreated; If not, they fail not to say, Ye are a little too Curious. Because *Men* have forged to themselves, that Women ought not to Study; they stand upon their Points, when Women demand to be informed of that which is Learned by Books. I esteem them Curious things; and regret, they have not the means to satisfie themselves therein; being often (only) hindered by a just Fear, to address themselves for that end, to touchy and foolish Heads; by whom they would find themselves jeer'd, instead of receiving Instruction. It seems to me, that Curiosity is one of the most certain Signes of a good Wit; that is, more capable of Learning. It is a Knowledge begun, which sets us forward, and makes us proceed farther in the way of Truth. When two Persons are touched by the same thing, and that the one looks upon it with Indifferency, and the other draws nearer, with designe to see it better; it is a mark, that this hath the Eyes more open. The Mind in both Sexes, is Equally fit for Sciences; and the Desire, which it may have of them, is no more to be blamed in the one, than in the other. When the Mind finds it self affected with a thing, which it sees but obscurely, it seems to be by a Natural Right, that it would be cleared therein: Ignorance being the most irksome Slavery (wherein it can be), it is as unreasonable to condemn a Person, who strives to get out of it; as a Wretch, who should endeavour to escape out of a Prison, where he were shut up.

Amongst all the Faults that Women are charged with, the Inconstant and Fickle Humour, is that which makes the maniest discontented. In the mean-time, they themselves are not less subject thereto; But because, they see themselves Masters, they think that every thing is lawful to them: And that Women, being once engaged to them, the knot ought to be indissoluble (onely) on their part; although that they be both Equal, and that every one is obliged for their own share.

They would not so often (Mutually) accuse one another of Levity, if they observed, that it is Natural to *Men;* and that, he that sayes Mortal, sayes Inconstant; and that, it is an Indispensible necessity of being, in the manner which we are made. We judge not of Objects, we love, or hate them not; but upon Appearances, which depend not on us. The same things appear to us diversly; sometime, because they have suffered some Alteration; some time, because we our selves are changed. The same Meat, more or less Seasoned, (Hot or Cold)[117] causeth in us quite different Sensations: And, remaining still the same, we are otherwise affected therewith in Sickness, than in Health. In our Infancy, we are indifferent, as to Things; which, ten Years after, we look upon with Passion, because the Body is changed.

If a *Woman* loves us, it is, Because she thinks us Lovely; and, if another hate us, it is, Because we appear to her Hateful. In one time we esteem those, whom we have slighted before; because they have not alwayes appeared to us the same; whether it be They, or We, who are Changed. And such an Object, being presented to the Heart, hath found the Door open; which, a Quarter of an Hour sooner or later, had been barr'd against it.

The Hovering, wherein we many times find our Selves betwixt two different Inclinations, which one and the same Object causeth in us, convinceth us in spight of our Teeth,[118] that the Passions are not free; and that we are unjust to complain, That we are otherwise considered of, than we would. As a small Matter is enough to kindle Love; so, a little thing can extinguish it: and that Passion depends no more upon us in its Progress, than in its Birth. Of ten Women, that aspire to be Loved, it falls out ordinarily, That she who hath least Merit, least of Birth and Beauty, shall carry it over the rest; because that she may have had a Brisker Air, or some-what more in Mode, or suitable to our Gusto,[119] in the Humour that then we find our selves in.

It is so far from doing wrong to Women, to accuse them of being more Cunning and Artificious than Men, that Men speak for them, if they know what they say; since, by so saying, they acknowledge them to be more Witty[120] and Prudent. Artifice is a secret way of attaining an End proposed, without being diverted: There is need of Wit, to find out that way; and Dexterity, to manage it: And we cannot find fault, that a Woman imployes Artifice, to avoyd being deceived. Craft is far more Pernicious, and more ordinary amongst Men: That hath alwayes been the common Road, to enter into the Places and Employments, where they may do greatest mischief.

And, instead of that, That *Men* (who have a mind to Cheat), employ their Goods, their Understanding, and their Power, from which we are rarely secure: *Women* have nothing to use, but Caresses and Eloquence, which are natural Means; against which, we may more easily guard our Selves, when there is any reason of Mistrust.

For the Summary of Accusation and Defect, it is said, That *Women* are more malitious and wicked than *Men:* And all the Evil, with which *Men* can charge *them,* is shut up in this Opinion. I do not believe, that those who entertain this Thought, do pretend, That there are more *Women* than *Men,* who do Mischief: That would be a manifest Falsehood; For, they have no part in Employments, and Charges; the abuse of which, is the cause of all publick Calamities; and their Vertue is too Exemplary; and the Disorders of *Men* too well known to call them in question.

When *Men* (then) say, That *Women* have more Malice; it signifies no more, but that, when they set themselves to do Evil, they do it more dextrously, and drive it farther than *Men.* Let it be so. This marks in them a most solid Advantage: For, one cannot be capable of doing much Mischief, without having good Judgement; and without being also (by Consequence) capable of doing much Good. So that, *Women* ought not to look upon this Reproach, more Injurious, than that which might be made to Rich and Powerful *Men;* that they are more wicked than the Poor, because they have more Opportunities of hurting: And *Women* might answer, as they; That, if they can do Hurt, they can also do Good; and that, if the Ignorance wherein they are left be the cause, Why they are worse than we; Knowledge, on the contrary, would render them much better.

This short Discussion, of the most signal Defects (which *Men* conceive peculiar, and natural, to the lovely *Sex*) proves two things; the one, That they are not so considerable, as the Vulgar Imagine; and the other, That they may be Rejected, upon the little Education which *Women* have; and what-ever they are, they may be amended by Instruction; of which, *Women* are no less capable than our Selves.

If the *Philosophers* had followed this Rule, in judging of all that concerns *Women,* they would have spoken more soundly; and had not (in Respect of them) fallen into Ridiculous Absurdities. But the most part, both of Antient and Modern, having only built their *Philosophy* upon popular Prejudices; and, having been in great Ignorance of themselves, it is no wonder, that they have so far mistaken others. Without giving our selves any trouble to medle with the Antients; we may say of the Modern, That the manner how they are Taught (making them believe, though falsely, That they cannot become more knowing, than those that have gone before them), renders them Slaves to Antiquity, and enclines them, to embrace (blindly) all that they find therein, as Constant and Universal Truths. And because, that all that they say against *Women,* is principally founded upon what they have Read in the Antients; it will not here be unprofitable, to relate some of the most curious Conceits on this Subject; which have been left to us, by these Illustrious Dead, whose very Ashes, and Rottenness, are at this Day, held in so great Veneration.

Plato (the Father of Antient *Philosophy)* thanked the Gods for three Favours, which they had bestowed on him; but chiefly, for that he was Born a *Man,* and not a *Woman.* If he had in his Eye their present Condition, I should easily be of his Mind: But that which makes me think, that he had some-what else in his Thoughts, is, The Doubt which he is said to have been often in, If *Women* ought to be placed in the Category of Beasts. That may be sufficient to Rational Men, to make him Condemn himself of Ignorance, or Brutishness; and totally to degrade him from the Title of *Divine,* which he enjoyes no more, but among Pedants.

His Scholar *Aristotle* (to whom the Schools still continue the Name of the Glorious Genius[121] of Nature; upon a Mistake, that he hath known her, better than any other *Philosopher*) pretends, that *Women* are but Monsters. Who would not believe it, upon the Authority of so Renowned a Personage? To say, It is an Impertinence; would be, to choak his Supposition too openly.

If a *Woman* (how Learned soever she might be), had wrote as much of *Men,* she would have lost all her Credit; and *Men* would have imagined it sufficient, to have refuted such a Foppery; by answering, That it must be a *Woman,* or a Fool, that had said so. In the mean-while, she would have no less Reason, than this *Philosopher. Women* are as Antient as *Men;* We see them in as great Number; and no *Man* is surprized to meet *them* in his Way. To be a Monster (according to the Opinion, it self, of that Man) there must be something

Extraordinary, and Surprizing. *Women* have nothing of all that: They have been alwayes made after the same Fashion; alwayes Pretty and Witty. And, if they be not made like *Aristotle*, they may say, That *Aristotle* was not made like *them*.

The Disciples of this Author (who lived in the time of *Philo*), fell into a Conceit, no less old Fashioned, in regard of *Women*; fancying to themselves (according to the Relation of that *Historian*), That they were Half-Men, or Imperfect Males. It is, without doubt, because they have not the Chin hung with a long beard; unless it be that, I can apprehend nothing. The *Two Sexes* (to be Perfect) ought to be, as we see *them*. If the one were altogether like the other, it would be neither of the *Two*. If *Men* be the fathers of *Women, Women* are the Mothers of *Men*; which, at least, renders them Equal: And we might have as much Reason, as these *Philosophers*, to say, That *Men* are Imperfect *Women*.

Socrates (who was the Morality and Oracle of Antiquity) speaking of the Beauty of that *Sex*; was accustomed to compare it to a Temple of a Fair Show, but built upon a Jakes.[122]

If this Conceit do not turn our Stomacks, we must only Laugh at it. It is probable,[123] that he judged of the Bodies of others, by his own, or by his Wives; who was a She-Devil, which made him detest her; and, that he spake of her *Sex*, to bring her down:[124] And, that he himself was mad to the very soul, because he was ugly as a Maggot.

Diogenes, Sir-named *The Dog*, because he was good at nothing but Biteing; seeing one day (in passing) two *Women*, who Discoursed together; told the Company, That there was two Serpents, an Aspe and a Viper, who Communicated to one another their Poison. That Saying is worthy of an Honest Man; and I wonder not, that it is Ranked among the goodly Philosophical Sentences. If the Wise *Men* of *Gottam*[125] had lived in his time, it is certain, we should have found their Ran-counters more sprightly. The good *Man* was a little wounded; and they that knew him a little, judged, that (at that time) he had nothing else to say.

For the admirable and pleasant *Democritus*; as he loved to be merry and laugh a little; we must not take every thing litterally which came from his Mouth. He was a very tall *Man*; and his Wife, one of the least: Being one day asked, Why he had so ill matched himself? He answered (according to his ordinary Rallery), That when we are obliged to choose, and when there is nothing that is good to be taken, the Least is alwayes the Best. If the same Question had been put to his Wife, she might have repartied with as much Reason; That a little and a big Husband, being both alike, the one as bad as the other, she had taken her's hap Hazzard; for fear, that if she had chosen, she might have done worse.

Cato (the Sage and Severe Critick) prayed often, That the Gods would pardon him, if he had been so Imprudent, as to trust the least Secret to a *Woman*. There stuck in the good *Mans* Mind, a Famous Passage in the *Roman* History; which Antiquaries use as a great Argument, to prove the little Secresie of *Women*: A Child of twelve Years of Age, being pressed by his Mother, to tell her the Resolution of the Senate (where he had been Assistant), invented to baffle her; that it had been decreed, That every Husband should have several Wives. Immediately, she went and told her Neighbours, to consult about her Measures with them; So that, in the space of half an Hour, it was all the Town over. I would gladly know, what a poor Husband would do, if in a State, where *Women* were the Mistresses (as in that of the *Amazones*); one should come and tell him, that it had been resolved in Counsel, That every Husband must have an Helper: without doubt, he would not open his Mouth.[126]

These are some of the great and sublime Conceits, which they (whom the Learned study as Oracles) have entertained, concerning the Beautiful *S E X*: And that which is pleasant, and odd, both together, is, That Grave *Men* seriously make use of that, which these Famous Antients have often but said in Drollery: So true it is, that Prejudices, and Pre-Occupation, do make *Men* themselves mistake the Mark, who pass for the most Rational, Judicious, and Wise.

F I N I S .

An Advertisement

*T*HE strongest Objections that can be made against us, are drawn from the Authority of great *Men*, and Holy *Scripture*: As to the former, We think to have sufficiently satisfied Them; by telling them, That we acknowledge no other Authority here, but that of Reason, and good Sense.

As to the *Scripture*; it is not at all contrary to the Intent of this *Treatise*, if we understand (well) both the one and the other. Here we pretend, That there is an intire Equallity betwixt the Two Sexes, being considered Independent of[127] Custom; which placeth often those of most Merit and Parts, in a Dependence on others. The *Scripture* speaketh not a word of Inequality: And, as the end of it is only to serve *Men* for a Rule in their Conduct, (according to the Notions which it gives of Justice); So, it leaves to every one the Liberty, to judge as well as he can of the natural (and true) state of Things. And, if we mind it, all the Objections which are drawn there-from, are but Sophisms of Prejudice; whereby sometimes, *Men* understand (of all *Women*) Passages, which only agree to some few in Particular: Sometime they refer to Nature, that which only flowes from Education or Custom, and that which sacred Authors have spoken with Relation to their own Times.

Textual Notes

All emendations from copy text and all instances where the English translation includes material not in the French are here included together with a sample of instances where the translation varies, deviates, or expressively renders the French original. Quotations from the French are all from the 1676 edition, page numbers to which are given parenthetically.

1. The translation here clearly follows the 1676 edition since the 1673 edition reads, "Il n'y a rien de plus délicat que de s'expliquer sur les femmes" (Sig. aii).
2. that in all] that all
3. render] renders
4. That is, "malcontented." "L'on n'ignore pas que ce discours sera beaucoup de mécontens" (Sig. a vi^v).
5. A variant form of "Trinkum," itself a "humorous alteration of trinket" (*OED*), often associated with women's trivial pursuits.
6. document] dotument
7. MONASTERIES] MONSASTERIES
8. Opinion] Opoinion
9. "comme un paradox singulier" (p. 5)
10. of] off
11. "les gens" (p. 9)
12. Sciences] Sciencies
13. advantage of Parts] advantage Parts
14. "un ordre general de l'Autheur de la Nature" (p. 13)
15. Whilst] Whil'st
16. "de la grossesse" (p. 17)
17. Interval] Intervenal
18. none were so] none so
19. "les particuliers" (p. 22)
20. Preference] Preferrence
21. contented] contentented
22. "ce n'a esté que pour éviter de tomber en guerre civile" (p. 26)

153

23. Extrinsical] Extrinseral   The French reads "exterieurs" (p. 31). See also *The Woman* pp. 104, 128 for *Extrinsical*.

24. them, in] them in

25. "à former l'esprit" (p. 36)

26. "quelque chose d'honneste" (p. 37)

27. are peculiar] are the peculiar

28. "les jeunes hommes au sortit de leurs études" (p. 38)

29. "posé" (p. 39)

30. to pump for the words] not in the French

31. of the age] not in the French

32. "précisément" (p. 44)

33. "des Lapidaires habiles" (p. 48)

34. let] lets

35. on] or [correction as per errata]

36. "le corps humain" (p. 57)

37. *Algebra*] *Alegebra*

38. are peculiar to] are the peculiar of

39. yielded] yeilded

40. "la science se doit uniquement rapporter à la vertue" (p. 63)

41. practised?] practised.

42. "la galerie des femmes fortes" (p. 63)

43. charge] change

44. "de leur Epoux" (p. 66)

45. application to the] application the

46. and Religion] not in the French

47. "c'est pour le reste de leur vie" (p. 69)

48. do] does

49. to their Years] not in the French

50. "et ceux qui n'en ont point" (p. 79)

51. yield] yeild

52. and other Flowers of Rhetorick] not in the French

53. known some] known, some

54. "les biens" (p. 87)

55. as much] asmuch

56. "gens d'esprit" (p. 98)

57. being no where to be found without their own Brains] not in the French

58. consists] consist

59. "les Nuances" (p. 107)

60. "Ciron" (p. 110)

61. affect] affects

62. they conform] they are conform

63. "de sciences differentes" (p. 120)

64. "sa langue naturelle" (p. 123)

65. "Cupidité" (p. 127)

66. Negotiations] Negoations

67. "Historiens" (p. 132)

68. "que Titelive & Quinte-curse" (p. 132)

69. Organ] Organs

70. "spirituels" (p. 141)

71. Life:] Life):
72. "l'esprit" (p. 148)
73. "l'imagination bizarre" (p. 144)
74. "On ne peut apprendre" (p. 149)
75. keeps] keep
76. looked] looked,
77. "AINSI il n'y a que le peu de lumiere" (p. 156)
78. Offices] Officers [correction as per errata]
79. at all] atall
80. were] be
81. Direct,] Direct
82. *Women*] *Woman*
83. "l'esprit" (p. 165)
84. "leur usages; qu'elle n'eust égard qu'au merite dans la distribution des charges; qu'elle ne mist dans les Emploies" (p. 166)
85. bad] bade
86. "luy mettre le vent, la poussiere, le Soleil en face" (p. 170)
87. "présidant à la teste d'un Parlement" (p. 170). Cotgrave, for "Parlement" gives: "a supreame, or soueragine Court, or Session, of Justice, established in the eight capitall Cities of France."
88. fortune] fortitude [following the French which reads "fortune" (p. 172)]
89. "elles leurs ont à l'égard des Emploies, égales en tout" (p. 172)
90. "spirituelles" (p. 174)
91. "la bonne foy" (p. 176)
92. "Imaginatives & spirituelles" (p. 178)
93. Advantage] Aadvantage
94. shed] shead   The French reads "de réprendre" (p. 181), for which Cotgrave gives "to resume, receive, take back . . . reprehend, blame, check, rebuke."
95. "broüillées" (p. 181)
96. in divers places] not in the French
97. "leurs sein" (p. 191)
98. "une Republique" (p. 196)
99. Material] Matterial
100. (in their Nature)] not in the French
101. make] makes
102. whither] whether
103. "faire les precieuses" (p. 211)
104. on] of
105. "que cette conduite" (p. 213)
106. it. When] it, when [following the French]
107. cry of a] cry a
108. such who] such in who
109. Sex so] Sex; so
110. "emportemens" (p. 216)
111. middle] midle
112. bad in another] bad another
113. "par leur esprit" (p. 218)
114. proper] propper
115. No parentheses in the French

116. "Nouvellistes" (p. 223)   The word is not in Cotgrave. The *OED* cites Shakespeare for "newsmonger."

117. (Hot or Cold)] not in the French

118. "malgré nous" (p. 229)

119. "goust" (p. 230), which Cotgrave gives as "taste."

120. "spirituelles" (p. 237)

121. Genius] Genious

122. "un gloaque" (p. 239)

123. probable] propable

124. "à dessein de la faire bouquer" (p. 239)

125. "Si Tobarin, Verboquet & l'Espregle" (p. 239)

126. "n'en diroit mot" (p. 242)

127. of Custom] of of Custom

Works Cited

For references to further studies that include discussions of Poullain de La Barre, see the bibliographies in *Corpus* 1, Alcover, Magné and Stock. Place of publication for early printed works is London unless otherwise indicated.

Works by Poullain de La Barre

[Poullain de La Barre, François?] *Les Rapports de la langue Latine avec la Françoise, pour traduire elegamment et sans peine.* Paris: Claude Thiboust et Pierre Escalassan, 1672.

Poullain de La Barre, François. *De l'education des Dames pour la conduite de l'esprit dans les sciences et dans les moeurs.* Paris: DuPuis, 1674. Rpt. Paris: Dezallier, 1679. Facsimile reprint, introduced by Bernard Magné. Toulouse: Université de Toulouse le Mirail, [1983].

———. *De l'egalité des deux sexes, Discours physique et moral, où l'on voit l'importance de se défaire des Préjugez.* Paris: DuPuis, 1673. Second printing 1676. "Seconde Edition" 1679. Facsimile reprint. Corpus des oeuvres de philosophie en langue française. Paris: Fayard, 1984.

———. *De l'excellence des Hommes, Contre l'egalité des sexes.* Paris: DuPuis, 1675.

———. *La Doctrine des protestants sur la liberté de lire l'Écriture Sainte.* Genève, 1720.

———. *Essai des remarques particulières sur la langue françoise pour la ville de Genève.* Genève, 1691.

Other Works Cited in the Introduction

Alcover, Madeleine. *Poullain de La Barre: Une aventure philosophique.* Biblio 17, vol. 1. Seattle: Papers on French Seventeenth-Century Literature, 1981.

Althusser, Louis. "Ideology and Ideological State Apparatuses." In *Lenin and Philosophy*, trans. Ben Bewster, 127–86. London: New Left Books, 1971.

Armogathe, Daniel. "De l'égalité des deux sexes, 'la belle question.'" *Corpus* 1(1985): 17–26.

à Wood, Anthony. *Athenae Oxonienses*. 2 vols. 1692.

Badinter, Elisabeth. "Ne portons pas trop loin la différence des sexes. . . ." *Corpus* 1(1985): 13–15.

Banks, John. *The Rival Kings*. 1677.

Barker, Francis. *The Tremulous Private Body: Essays in Subjection*. London: Methuen, 1984.

Barret, Michèle. "Ideology and the Cultural Production of Gender." In Judith Newton and Deborah Rosenfelt, eds., *Feminist Criticism and Social Change: Sex, Class and Race in Literature and Culture*, 65–85. London: Methuen, 1985.

————. *Women's Oppression Today: Problems in Marxist Feminist Analysis*. London: Verso, 1980.

Battestin, Martin. *The Providence of Wit*. Oxford: Clarendon Press, 1974.

Baxter, Richard. *Naked Popery; Or, The Naked Falsehood of a Book Called the Catholic Naked Truth*. 1677.

Beauvoir, Simone de, *The Second Sex*. Trans. H. M. Parshley. New York: Knopf, 1953.

Behn, Aphra. *Abdelazer; Or, The Moor's Revenge*. 1677.

————. *The Counterfeit Bridegroom*. 1677.

————. *The Debauchee*. 1677.

————. *The Rover, Or, The Banisht Cavaliers*. 1677.

————. *The Town Fopp: Or, Sir Timothy Tawdrey*. 1677.

Blanchard, Rae. "Richard Steele and the Status of Women." *Studies in Philology* 36(1929): 325–55.

The British Library General Catalogue of Printed Books to 1975. 360 vols. London: Bingley and Saur, 1979–1987.

Burnet, Gilbert. *History of His Own Times*. 2 vols. 1724–1734.

Burnet, Thomas. *The Theory of the Earth: Containing an Account of the Original of the Earth. And of all the General Changes Which it hath already undergone, Or is to undergo Till the Consummation of Things*. 1684. Reprint. Carbondale, Il.: Southern Illinois University Press, 1965.

Cockburn, Catherine Trotter. *The Revolution of Sweden*. 1706.

Collier, Mary. *The Woman's Labour; an Epistle to Mr. Stephen Duck*. 1739. Reprinted, introduced by Moira Ferguson, in *"The Thresher's Labour" and "The Woman's Labour."* Augustan Reprint Society no. 230. Los Angeles: William Andrews Clark Memorial Library, University of California, 1985.

Collins, Francis, ed. *The Registers and Monumental Inscriptions of Charterhouse Chapel*. London: Harleian Society, 1892.

Common Sense: Or, The Englishman's Journal 135 (1 September 1739).

Conway, Anne. *The Conway Letters: The Correspondence of Anne, Viscountess Conway, Henry More, and Their Friends, 1642–1684*. Ed. Marjorie Hope Nicolson. New Haven: Yale University Press, 1930.

Cotgrave, Randle. *A Dictionarie of the French and English Tongues*. 1611. Reprint introduced by William S. Woods. Columbia: University of South Carolina Press, 1950. Reprint 1968.

Crawford, Patricia. "Womens' Published Writings 1600–1700." In *Women in English Society 1500–1800*, ed. Mary Prior, 211–82. London: Methuen, 1985.

Cross, Claire. "'He-Goats before the Flocks': A Note on the Part Played by Women in the Founding of Some Civil War Churches." In *Popular Belief and Practice*, ed. G. J. Cuming and Derek Baker, 195–202. Studies in Church History, vol. 8. Cambridge: Cambridge University Press, 1972.

[Curll, Edmund]. *The History of the English Stage, from the Restauration to the Present Times.* "By Mr. Thomas Betterton." 1741.

Davies, Kathleen M. "The Sacred Condition of Equality—How Original Were Puritan Doctrines of Marriage?" *Social History* 5(1977): 563–80.

The Disorders of Love. Truly expressed In the Unfortunate Amours of Givry Mademoiselle de Guise. 1677.

[Drake, Judith?] *See* "An Essay."

Dryden, John. *All For Love: or, The World Well Lost.* 1678.

———. Preface to *Ovid's Epistles, Translated by Several Hands* [1680]. In *"Of Dramatic Poesy" and Other Critical Essays.* Ed. George Watson. 2 vols. London: Dent, 1962. Reprint. 1967.

———. *The State of Innocence.* 1677.

———. *Tyrannick Love.* 1670.

Du Bosc, Jacques. *The Accomplish'd Woman.* Trans. Walter Montague. 1656.

———. *The Compleat Woman.* Trans. N. N. 1639.

———. *The Excellent Woman Described by Her True Characteristics and Their Opposites.* Attributed to Theophilus Dorrington. 1692.

———. *L'Honneste Femme.* Paris, 1600.

———. *The Secretary of Ladies. Or, A new collection of letters and answers composed by Moderne Ladies and Gentlemen.* Attributed to Theophilus Dorrington. 1638.

Duck, Stephen. "The Thresher's Labour." In *Poems on Several Occasions.* 1736. Reprinted, introduced by Moira Ferguson, in *"The Thresher's Labour" and "The Woman's Labour."* Augustan Reprint Society no. 230. Los Angeles: William Andrews Clark Memorial Library, University of California, 1985.

Dunn, Catherine M. "The Changing Image of Woman in Renaissance Society and Literature." In *What Manner of Woman: Essays in English and American Life and Literature*, ed. Marlene Springer, 15–38. New York: New York University Press, 1977.

L'École des filles, ou la philosophie des dames, divisée en deux dialogues, agere et pati. Paris, 1655.

An Essay In Defence of the Female Sex. 3d ed., attributed to Judith Drake. 1696.

Evelyn, Mary. *See Mundus Muliebris.*

Fauré, Christine. "Poullain de La Barre, sociologue et libre penseur." *Corpus* 1(1985): 43–49.

Ferguson, Moira. *First Feminists: British Women Writers, 1578–1799.* Bloomington: Indiana University Press, 1985.

Foxon, David. *Libertine Literature in England 1660–1745.* [Reprinted, with revisions, from *Book Collector* 12(1963) 21–36, 159–77, 294–307, 476–87.] London: Book Collector, 1964.

Fraisse, Geneviève. "Poullain de La Barre, ou le procès des préjugeés." *Corpus* 1(1985): 27–41.

Goreau, Angeline. *Reconstructing Aphra: A Social Biography of Aphra Behn.* New York: Dial, 1980.

Hearne, Samuel. *Domus Carthusiana: Or an Account of the most Noble Foundation of the Charter-House.* 1677.

Henderson, Katherine Usher, and Barbara F. McManus, eds. *Half Humankind: Contexts and Texts of the Controversy about Women in England 1540-1640.* Urbana: University of Illinois Press, 1985.

Hill, Christopher. *The World Turned Upside Down: Radical Ideas during the English Revolution.* New York: Viking, 1972.

Hine, Ellen McNiven. "The Woman Question in Early Eighteenth-Century French Literature: The Influence of François Poulain de La Barre." *Studies on Voltaire and the Eighteenth Century* 116(1973): 65–79.

Hull, Suzanne W. *Chaste, Silent, and Obedient: English Books for Women, 1475-1640.* San Marino, CA: Huntington Library, 1982.

Hunt, Margaret. "Hawkers, Bawlers, and Mercuries: Women and the London Press in the Early Enlightenment." *Women and History* 9(1984): 41–68.

Hunter, Michael. *Science and Society in Restoration England.* Cambridge: Cambridge University Press, 1981.

Jardine, Lisa. *Still Harping on Daughters: Women and Drama in the Age of Shakespeare.* Brighton, UK: Harvester, 1983.

Josselin, Ralph. *The Diary of Ralph Josselin 1616-1683.* Ed. Alan MacFarlane. London: Oxford University Press, 1976.

Kelly, Joan. "Early Feminist Theory and the *Querelle des Femmes*, 1400-1789." *Signs* 8(1982): 4–28.

Kra, Pauline. "Montesquieu and Women." In *French Women and the Age of Enlightenment*, ed. Samia I. Spencer, 272–84. Bloomington: Indiana University Press, 1985.

L., A., *An Impartial and full Account of the Life and Death of the Unhappy Lord Russel, Eldest Son and Heir of the Present Earl of Bedford, who was Executed for High Treason, July 21, 1683.* 1684.

———. *An Inducement to the Intrenching of the City of York.* 1642.

———. *A Question Deeply concerning Married Persons, and such as intend to Marry.* 1653.

———. *A true relation of the late expedition of . . . the Earl of Ormond.* 1642.

———. *To all the honest, wise and grave citizens of London.* 1648.

L., A., trans. *The Interiour Christian: or The interiour conformity; which Christians ought to have with Jesus Christ*, by Jean de Bernières Louvigny Antwerp [London?], 1684.

———, trans. *A Letter from a French Lawyer.* 1689.

———, trans. *Reflections Upon Ancient and Modern History*, by Renée Rapin. 1678.

[L., A.], trans. *Elenchus Motuum Nuperorum in Anglia: Or, A short Historical Account of the Rise and Progress of the Late Troubles in England*, by George Bate. 1685. "Second Edition." 1688.

La Calprenède. *Pharamond.* Trans. John Philips. 1677.

Lainé, Pierre. *The Princely Way to the French Tongue, As it was first compiled For the Use of Her Highness The Lady Mary, And since taught Her Royal Sister the Lady Anne.* 1667.

La Roche-Guilhem, Anne de. *Almanzaïde.* Paris, 1676.

———. *Almanzor and Almazida.* 1678.

————. *Asteria and Tamberlain*. 1677.

————. *Histoire des Favorites*. 1697.

————. *The History of Female Favourites*. 1772.

————. *Journal Amoureux d'Espagne*. "Cologne" [Amsterdam], 1675.

————. *Rare en Tout: Comedie*. 1677.

Latt, David J. "Praising Virtuous Ladies: The Literary Image and Historical Reality of Women in Seventeenth-century England." In *What Manner of Women: Essays in English and American Life and Literature*, ed. Marlene Springer, 39–64. New York: New York University Press, 1977.

Lee, Nathaniel. *The Rival Queens, Or The Death of Alexander the Great*. 1677.

Le Moyne, Pierre. *La Gallerie des Femmes fortes*. Paris, 1647.

————. *The Gallery of Heroick Women*. Trans. Marquesse of Winchester. 1652.

Levine, David. *Family Formation in an Age of Nascent Capitalism*. New York: Academic, 1977.

Levingston, Anne. *The State of the Case in brief between the Countess of Sterling and others, by Petition in Parliament, Plaintiffs; and M^{ris} Levingston, Defendent*. 1654.

————. *A true Narrative of the Case so much controverted between A. Levingston . . . and others*. 1655.

Lloyd, William. *Papists No Catholicks: And Popery no Christianity*. 1677.

Lovell, Archibald. *A Summary of Material Heads Which may be Enlarged and Improved into a Compleat Answer To Dr. Burnet's Theory of the Earth*. 1696.

————, trans. *The Comical History of the States and Empires of the Worlds of the Moon and Sun*, by Cyrano de Bergerac. 1687.

————, trans. *Conversations of the Mareschal of Clerambault and the Chevalier de Méré*, by Antoine Gombaud Méré. 1677.

————, trans. *The Critical History of the Religions and Customs of the Eastern Nations*, by Richard Simons. 1685.

————, trans. *An Historical Treatise Of The Foundation and Prerogatives of the Church of Rome*, by Louis Maimbourg. 1685.

————, trans. *Indiculus Universalis; Or, The universe in Epitome, wherein the Names of almost all the Works of Nature, of all Arts and Sciences, with their most necessary Terms, are in English, Latine & French, Methodically and distinctly digested*, by François Antoine Pomey. 1679.

————, trans. *The Military Duties of the Officers of Cavalry, Containing the way of exercising the Horse, According to the practise of this present time*, by ———— de La Fontaine. 1678.

————, trans. *The Travels of Monsieur de Thévenot Into the Levant*, by Jean de Thévenot. 1687.

————, trans. *A Treatise Concerning the Motion of the Seas and Winds*, by Isaac Vossius. 1676.

————, trans. *A Treatise of Lithotomy: Or, of the Extraction of the Stone out of the Bladder*, by François Tolet. 1683.

[Lovell, Archibald], trans. *The Count de Gabalis*, by Nicolas de Montfaucon de Villars. 1680.

MacDonald, Michael. *Mystical Bedlam: Madness, Anxiety, and Healing in Seventeenth-Century England*. Cambridge: Cambridge University Press, 1981.

MacLean, Ian. *The Renaissance Notion of Woman*. Cambridge: Cambridge University Press, 1980.

Madan, F. F. *Milton, Salmasius, and Dugard*. London: Oxford Bibliographical Society, 1923.

Magné, Bernard. "Le féminisme de Poullain de La Barre, origine et signification." Ph.D. diss., University of Toulouse, 1964.

Marvell, Andrew. *An Account of the Growth of Popery, And Arbitrary Government in England*. Amsterdam, 1677.

Medley [pseud.] "Sophia, A Lady Of Quality." *Notes and Queries* 8th Ser. 11(1897): 348.

Miller, John. *Popery and Politics in England, 1660–1688*. Cambridge: Cambridge University Press, 1973.

Moore, C. A. "The First of the Militants in English Literature." *Nation* 102 (1916): 194–96.

Moureau, François. "Autour du mythe de la femme: Une réfutation inconnue de Poullain de La Barre." *Cahiers de littérature du dix-septième siècle* 2(1980): 89–94.

Mundus Foppiensis: Or, The Fop Display'd. Being the Ladies Vindication, In Answer to a late Pamphlet. 1691.

Mundus Muliebris: Or, The Ladies Dressing-Room Unlocked, And her Toilette Spread. In Burlesque. Together with the Fop-Dictionary, Compiled for the Use of the Fair Sex. Attributed to Mary Evelyn. 1690.

A Narrative of the Great and Bloody Fight Between the Prince of Orange and the Duke of Orleans The King of Frances General, Near the City of St. Omers, On Sunday the first of April 1677. with the Numbers of the Kil'd and Wounded Men. Being an Impartial Account. 1677.

"A new Method for making Women as useful and as capable of maintaining themselves, as the Men are; and consequently preventing their becoming old Maids, or taking ill Courses. By a Lady." *Gentleman's Magazine* 9(1739): 525–6.

Nicolson, Marjorie Hope. *Mountain Gloom and Mountain Glory*. Ithaca: Cornell University Press, 1959.

Nouvelle biographie générale depuis les temps les plus reculés jusqu'a nos jours. Paris: Didot, 1886.

Nussbaum, Felicity. *The Brink of All We Hate: Social Satires on Women 1660–1750*. Lexington: University of Kentucky Press, 1984.

———, ed. *Satires on Women*. Augustan Reprint Society no 180. Los Angeles: William Andrews Clark Memorial Library, University of California, 1976.

Ogg, David. *England in the Reign of Charles the Second*. 2d ed. Oxford: Clarendon, 1956. Reprint. 1967.

Ozment, Steven. *When Fathers Ruled: Family Life in Reformation Europe*. Cambridge: Harvard University Press, 1983.

Pepys, Samuel. *The Diary of Samuel Pepys*. Ed. Robert Latham and William Matthews. 11 vols. Berkeley and Los Angeles: University of California Press, 1970–83.

Perry, Ruth. "Mary Astell's Response to the Enlightenment." *Women and History* 9(1984): 13–40.

Pope, Alexander. *"The Rape of the Lock" and Other Poems*, ed. Geoffrey Tillotson. London: Methuen, 1940.

Powell, Chilton L. *English Domestic Relations 1487–1653: A Study of Matrimony and Family Life in Theory and Practice As Revealed by the Literature, Law, and History of the Period*. New York: Columbia University Press, 1917.

Prior, Mary. "Women and the Urban Economy: Oxford 1500–1800." In *Women in English Society 1500–1800*, ed. Mary Prior, 93–117. London: Methuen, 1985.

———, ed. *Women in English Society 1500–1800*. London: Methuen, 1985.

Reynolds, Myra. *The Learned Lady in England, 1650–1760*. Boston: Houghton Mifflin, 1920.

Rogers, Daniel. *Matrimoniall Honour: Or, The mutuall Crowne and comfort of godly, loyall, and chaste Marriage*. 1642.

Rogers, Katherine. *Feminism in Eighteenth-Century England*. Urbana: University of Illinois Press, 1982.

Scudéri, Madeleine de. *Almahide*. Trans. John Philips. 1677.

Sedley, Charles, *Antony and Cleopatra*. 1677.

———. *The Poetical and Dramatic Works of Sir Charles Sedley*. 2 vols. Ed. V. de Sola Pinto. London: Constable, 1928.

Seidel, Michael. "Poullain de La Barre's *The Woman As Good as the Man.*" *Journal of the History of Ideas* 35(1974): 499–508.

Shepherd, Simon, ed. *The Woman's Sharp Revenge: Five Women's Pamphlets from the Renaissance*. New York: St. Martins, 1985.

Smith, Florence. *Mary Astell*. New York: Columbia University Press, 1916.

Smith, Hilda. *Reason's Disciples: Seventeenth-Century English Feminists*. Urbana: University of Illinois Press, 1982.

Sophia [pseud.] *Beauty's Triumph: Or, The Superiority of the Fair Sex invincibly proved*. 1751.

———. *Man Superior to Woman: Or, A Vindication of Man's Natural Right of Sovereign Authority Over the Woman*. 1739.

———. *Woman Not Inferior to Man: Or, A short and modest Vindication of the natural Right of the Fair-Sex to a perfect Equality of Power, Dignity, and Esteem, with the Men*. 1739.

Spencer, Samia I., ed. *French Women and the Age of Enlightenment*. Bloomington: Indiana University Press, 1985.

Sprat, Thomas. *History of the Royal Society*. 1667.

Springer, Marlene, ed. *What Manner of Women: Essays in English and American Life and Literature*. New York: New York University Press, 1977.

Spufford, Margaret. *Small Books and Pleasant Histories: Popular Fiction and Its Readership in Seventeenth-Century England*. Athens, GA: University of Georgia Press, 1981.

Stock, Marie-Louise. "Poullain de La Barre: A Seventeenth-Century Feminist." Ph.D. diss., Columbia University, 1961.

Tate, Nahum. *A Present For the Ladies: Being a Historical Vindication of the Female Sex*. 1692.

Thomas, Keith. "The Double Standard." *Journal of the History of Ideas* 20(1959): 195–216.

———. "Women and the Civil War Sects." *Past and Present* 13(1958): 42–62. Reprinted in *Crisis in Europe, 1560–1660*, ed. Trevor Aston, 317–40. London: Routledge & Kegan Paul, 1965. Reprint. 1970.

Thompson, Roger. *Unfit for Modest Ears*. London: MacMillan, 1979.

Tilney, Edmund. *A brief and pleasant discourse of duties in Mariage; called the Flower of Frendshippe*. 1568.

Upham, A. H. "English *Femmes Savantes* at the End of the Seventeenth Century." *Journal of English and Germanic Philology* 12(1913): 262–76.

Venn, John and J. A. Venn. *Alumni Cantabrigienses. Pt. 1, From the Earliest Times to 1751*. 4 vols. Cambridge: Cambridge University Press, 1922–24. Nendeln, Liechtenstein: Kraus Reprint, 1974.

Vernon, Paul F. Introduction to *The Rival Queens*, by Nathaniel Lee. Lincoln: University of Nebraska Press, 1970.

Walsh, William. *A Dialogue Concerning Women, Being a Defence of the Sex*. 1691.

Willey, Basil. *Eighteenth-Century Background*. London: Chatto & Windus, 1949.

———. Introduction to *Theory of the Earth*, by Thomas Burnet. Carbondale, IL: Southern Illinois University Press, 1965.

Williams, Ethyn Morgan. "Women Preachers in the Civil Wars." *Journal of Modern History* 1(1929): 561–69.

Williamson, Marilyn. Introduction to *The Female Poets of Great Britain*, ed. Frederic Rowton. 1853. Reprint. Detroit: Wayne State University Press, 1981.

Wing, Donald, et al., eds. *Short-Title Catalogue of Books Printed in England, Scotland, Ireland, Wales, and British America and of English Books Printed in Other Countries, 1641–1700*. 2d ed. 2 vols. to date. New York: Modern Language Association, 1972–.

Woodbridge, Linda. *Women and the English Renaissance: Literature and the Nature of Womankind, 1540–1620*. Urbana: University of Illinois Press, 1984.

Wortley Montagu, Lady Mary. *The Nonsense of Common Sense* 6 (24 January 1738). Reprinted in *Essays and Poems and "Simplicity a comedy" by Lady Wortley Montague*, ed. Robert Halsband and Isobel Grundy, 130–34. Oxford: Clarendon Press, 1977.

Wright, Louis B. *Middle-Class Culture in Elizabethan England*. Chapel Hill: University of North Carolina Press, 1935.

Wrightson, Keith. *English Society, 1580–1680*. London: Hutchinson, 1982.

Wycherley, William. *The Plays of William Wycherley*. Ed. Arthur Friedman. Oxford: Clarendon Press, 1979.

After graduating from Jesus College, Cambridge, Gerald MacLean taught in Canada, Greece and Libya before taking his Ph.D. at the University of Virginia. He is currently assistant professor of English at Wayne State University. In addition to several articles on seventeenth-century poetry and feminist critical theory, Dr. MacLean is the author of the forthcoming *Time's Witness: Historical Representation in English Poetry, 1603–60*. In addition to editing the English poems commemorating the Stuart Restoration, he is writing a book "The Living Memory: Studies in English Popular Culture, 1642–1984."

The manuscript was prepared for publication by Michael Lane. The book was designed by Joanne Elkin Kinney. The typeface for the text is Times Roman. The display types are Cancelleresca Bold and Times Roman. The book is printed on 55-lb. Glatfelter text paper. The cloth edition is bound in ICG Linen.

Manufactured in the United States of America.